Devil's Canyon Double Cross

DEVIL'S CANYON DOUBLE CROSS

CLIFFORD BLAIR

AVALON BOOKS
THOMAS BOUREGY AND COMPANY, INC.
401 LAFAYETTE STREET
NEW YORK, NEW YORK 10003

PRINTED IN THE UNITED STATES OF AMERICA
BY HADDON CRAFTSMEN, SCRANTON, PENNSYLVANIA

To my parents, Dr. Clifford J. and Larue Blair, with deepest love and gratitude for their unceasing love, encouragement, and support.

Prologue

As he reined in at the mouth of the canyon, Steve Lawton thought that he was probably riding into a trap.

Somewhere in the brush-choked confines of the canyon, Zeke Spurd, his quarry, was probably waiting to practice his talent for bushwhacking. It was this talent that had sent Spurd on the run and put Steve on his trail. And the barren granite walls of this canyon, Steve knew from bitter experience, offered a multitude of sites for a hunted man to wait in concealment to turn the tables on his tracker.

Steve's wiry Indian paint stallion sidestepped a little, as if sensing his owner's unease. "Quiet, Traveler," Steve murmured, and sat a moment longer to contemplate the jumbled terrain of jagged stone and tangled brush before him.

Cañon del Diablo was what the old Spaniards had called this mile-and-a-half-long rift in the harsh peaks of the Wichita Mountains. Canyon of the Devil. The name had stuck down through the centuries since those first conquistadores had crossed this land in search of gold and conquest. Even then, Steve supposed, these low, rugged mountains must have been a haven for the outcasts and the hunted—survivors of Indian tribes slaughtered by the

1

Spaniards, deserters from the ranks of the Spanish invaders themselves.

Now a part of the recently opened Oklahoma Territory, the Wichitas were still known as the province and refuge of wanted outlaws and hunted killers, of renegade whites and Indians. It was a no-man's-land where the law was what the strong made it.

A mile and a half from where Steve sat the paint, the canyon emptied into the north fork of the Red River, but between that spot and this lay the tortured terrain that, over the decades, had spawned tales of doomed men and hidden gold. There were old-timers who swore that the faces of the canyon walls changed from one day to the next, shifting and sliding in such an unnatural fashion as could drive men mad and, at the very least, prevent them from retracing their steps to the same spot twice in a row. The devil himself, they would tell you, had been the architect of this canyon.

Steve loosened his Winchester in its saddle sheath. He had halted in the shadow of a granite overhang, both to be out of the rays of the blistering noontime sun and out of the sight of any watcher from within the canyon. Still, it seemed now, he felt some eerie gaze touch him like the waft of a cold breeze from the mouth of a cavern.

He had come out of the territorial capital of Guthrie some three days before, hard on the trail of Zeke Spurd. Spurd had made the mistake of letting himself be seen when, shooting from ambush, he had killed the latest of his robbery-murder victims in the area of Guthrie. But a cowhand searching for strays had witnessed the act, recognized Spurd, and, escaping the killer's rifle, had reported the murder in time for Steve to get on Spurd's trail while it was yet fresh.

Knowing he was hunted, Spurd had proven a wily and elusive prey, heading southwest for the lawless sanctuary of the Wichitas, where, Steve was certain, he planned to make a stand. Steve had actually had him in sight when he plunged into the brush of Devil's Canyon and disappeared. It had taken Steve an hour to reach the site over the intervening terrain, and he now sat and sweated and considered his choices.

Driven to violent desperation by the relentless pursuit, Spurd was probably concealed somewhere above on the cliff wall, waiting for Steve to pass within range of his deadly rifle. And Spurd, Steve recalled, favored an old Sharps buffalo gun for his work. Riding into that canyon as target for an expert marksman intent on killing him from cover was not a pleasant prospect.

Steve sighed. If he took the time to circle over the rough ground and enter the canyon from its far end, he would still be exposing himself to a concealed gun. Besides, without having some idea of Spurd's location, there was no way to try to get behind or above the bushwhacker. That left only one tactic, and it was risky at best. But, then, there was never a sure way of going up against a hidden gun.

He would have to ride down the canyon, staying to the cover of the brush and the shadows of the canyon walls, and hope to draw Spurd's fire. Once the killer had betrayed his location by firing, it would be a whole new setup, Steve hoped.

The searing sun was directly overhead in a cloudless sky turned almost silver by its glare. He needed to wait an hour, perhaps two, until the sun was lower in the sky and the concealing shadows of the canyon walls were longer, before he tried to ride under Spurd's gun.

Steve swung his right leg over the saddle horn and slid out of the saddle—an old trick, and habitual with him now, that left a man's hands free as he dismounted and kept him from having to offer his back as an open target. Absently his fingers flicked over the butt of the unadorned Colt .45 that hung at his waist, and brushed the hilt of the heavy bowie knife sheathed on his left for a cross draw.

He loosened his stallion's girth, and the wiry animal settled into a hipshot stance in the still heat. The shade of the overhang where he had halted was as good a place to wait as any. He drank sparingly from one of his canteens, then filled his Stetson for the paint. Traveler was grateful for the refreshment. Even though descended from Indian mustangs, with the sure-footed stamina inherent to the breed, the paint had found traveling the Wichitas no easy trek.

"Take a rest, Traveler," Steve told the animal softly. He put the Stetson back on his head, and then he pivoted fast as something—an inhalation of breath, a whisper of a foot on stone, or sheer feral instinct—warned him of danger.

"Cazador, you are still good," said the ancient Indian who had seemingly materialized from the canyon wall behind him. "You still have the blood of the hunter—*el cazador.*"

Steve let the tension ease out of his muscles slowly. "Velador," he greeted the newcomer with a slight nod of his head.

The old Indian stepped forward, and his mouth curled in an expression that only his ageless eyes defined as a smile rather than a snarl. Velador had changed little in the years since Steve had last seen him. His shoulders, stooped with unguessable age, gave the impression of a former height greater than was common among Indians. His hairless torso, only partially concealed by a leather vest, was all gnarled muscle and dried copper skin stretched taut across gaunt ribs and a washboard middle. The ugly black tattoo of some vaguely reptilian creature encircled his chest as if he were entrapped in its coils.

Above that fleshless torso was a wrinkled leather mask of a face, the dark crevices of which spoke of age and wisdom and hard experience. The eyes were black and deep and seemed at times to penetrate like iron rods and at others to draw like magnets. A long mane of dead silver hair, streaked with the black of a long-ago youth, framed Velador's face and fell straight to his shoulders, pulled back behind his ears by a rawhide thong.

He came forward with the stiff shuffle of an arthritic, and Steve wondered, not for the first time, how the old brave was able to move among the barren rocks with such uncanny silence.

"It has been much time since I have seen you." Velador halted in front of him, and Steve did not have to look down much to meet those onyx eyes.

"I am no longer with the Rangers," Steve explained.

"Huuh." Velador nodded as if he understood, and lowered himself stiffly into a cross-legged sitting position. Steve followed suit, and the old Indian regarded him solemnly. "But you are still hunting," he said. "Still hunting men."

"Sometimes," Steve said. "But only as a favor to the United States deputy marshal over at Guthrie."

Velador nodded again. "Heck Thomas. He is a good man."

Steve noted that the flint head of the old-style tomahawk Velador carried slung at his waist was honed to almost a razor's edge, a considerable accomplishment on a stone ax. He guessed that the blade of the old bowie knife sheathed opposite it was also in excellent condition. Other than these implements, Velador carried no weapons, although Steve recalled having seen the old brave in possession of both a bow and a battered Winchester when he had encountered him in the past among these lonely crags.

"I have a place outside of Guthrie now," Steve went on. "I staked a claim to it during the land run a couple of years back."

The leathery features seemed to darken ominously. "I have heard of this thing. Hundreds, thousands of white men racing like hungering wolves to claim the lands once promised to my people. It is not good. Always the white men want more and then more, and always they spread like devouring grasshoppers across the land."

Steve nodded. "What you say is true," he said, and meant it. Indians like Velador were a rarity these days in the very lands where, not so many decades ago, they had reigned supreme. "But a man has need of a home." He felt the uncomfortable urge to defend whatever his own role might have been in the expulsion of the red man from his native lands. "Just as these mountains are your home."

"My home," Velador repeated softly. He seemed to muse about distant places and times. "It is not good for white men to come into these mountains," he said after a moment, and his voice, louder, possessed a curious strength. "There are evils here that the white men do not understand, Cazador, not even you." His black eyes glinted strangely. "Dark spirits guard the secrets of these mountains, and they will suck the life from those who seek to uncover those secrets."

That eerie cold breeze seemed to brush Steve's neck

again there in the summer heat. "I am not after the mountains' secrets," he said. "Only a man, a bad man. A killer who shoots from ambush and then robs those he has killed. I have followed him here to *el Cañon del Diablo*."

"I know," Velador said. "I watched him come. He waits for you now up ahead to kill you as you say he has killed others. There is a path that will let you get above him without being seen. I will show it to you."

"Thank you," Steve said.

"I show you so that you can take him and leave these mountains."

Steve nodded. "This I will do."

Velador levered himself to his feet with difficulty, and his first steps were awkward. He led Steve to a pile of boulders which must have sloughed away from the canyon wall in some age past. "There." He pointed with a bony hand that did not tremble in the least. "That is where the trail begins. Follow it along the rim of the canyon. Three hundred yards from here you will find him below you on a ledge on the canyon wall."

Steve took a few steps past him, gazing hard at the stone debris. He could make out the faint signs of a trail, one used undoubtedly mostly by beasts and an occasional man.

"Remember the dark spirits, Cazador," came the Indian's voice from behind him. "Go carefully, in your way."

"I'll let the Good Lord protect me from the dark spirits," Steve began as he turned back from the beginning of the trail. Then he froze. Velador was gone. Traveler stood alone in the shade of the overhang.

Steve shook his head. He was glad it was not Velador he hunted among these ancient peaks.

Returning to Traveler, he drew the Winchester from its

sheath and recalled his earlier feeling of unseen eyes watching him. The old Indian haunted these mountains like one of the dark spirits of which he spoke.

Steve ventured onto the trail, finding it necessary at times to claw his way up sections of sun-heated stone that seared the callused flesh of his palms. Finally he emerged cautiously from clinging thorns to find himself positioned at the rim of the canyon. Its rugged wall dropped away to brush and rock below.

He cat-footed forward, silent in the knee-high Apache moccasins that he wore. They were not meant for riding a horse, but for this business of stalking a man, there was no better footwear.

The going was easier now, although he still had to by-pass or ease through occasional thickets of thorny brush. He paused frequently to scan the canyon below him, and as he neared the distance specified by the old brave, he dropped to his belly and went forward along the very edge on knees and elbows, Winchester gripped in front of his face.

Movement drew his eye, and he went motionless, eyes narrowing. Velador was as good as his word. Steve had found his prey. Spurd knelt on a narrow ledge ahead of him, some thirty feet down the cliff face. A coiled lariat showed how Spurd had gained the site, and as Steve watched, the outlaw repeated the movement that had drawn his attention. As if sighting on a target, Spurd lifted his huge old Sharps to his shoulder, lowered it, then snapped it up again. The ledge gave Spurd an open view of a clear section of the canyon floor, and Steve felt thankful that he had not had to ride under the barrel of that waiting Sharps. He owed Velador for this.

Silently, aware now of his heartbeat, sweat, and the

scent of dust in his nostrils, Steve snaked forward until he was closer to the waiting outlaw. He did not want to be positioned directly above Spurd; shooting down from that point would be too awkward. When he was satisfied with the angle, he eased up into a kneeling position and put the Winchester's sights on Spurd's faded red shirt. It made a nice target.

"That's all, Zeke," he shouted. "It's over. Drop that buffalo gun."

Along the barrel of the Winchester he could see Spurd stiffen, and he let his finger tighten on the Winchester's trigger. "Dead drop, Zeke," he added. "You wouldn't even have time for a prayer. But it's your choice."

Slowly, the darkly stubbled face turned back and up toward him.

"No need to look, Zeke. Just do as I say. Drop the Sharps. Toss it over the edge."

"Blast you, Lawton!" Spurd's voice carried clearly as he spotted Steve's kneeling figure. "What kind of man would make me smash a rifle like this?"

"One who wants to stay alive. Okay, I'm through talking. Drop it or I drop you."

Spurd let his shoulders sag in defeat and started to straighten. Then he was spinning tight and fast, swinging the buffalo gun as he turned. But the huge old rifle was too heavy for gunfighting or snap shots. Steve felt his teeth grind hard together as he tightened his finger the rest of the way on the Winchester's trigger.

The shot bounced echoes up and down Devil's Canyon. Spurd was knocked back around. The Sharps flew from his hands and sailed out of sight over the rim of the ledge. Spurd collapsed in a twisted heap. Steve straightened to his full height, rifle at waist level now, barrel angled down toward the bushwhacker.

Steve gave a long sigh as he saw the outlaw flop over onto his back, a dark stain showing high up on his red shirt. Spurd still lived. Steve had not wanted to kill, but when your prey turned, there was no way you could ever really pick your shots.

Spurd stared up at him, anger and pain mingling on his coarse features. "I told you I had a dead drop, Zeke," Steve said. "You made the choice." He shook his head wearily. "Now I have to get you up from there."

Chapter One

"**N**ow that we're back in town, get me to a doctor!" Zeke Spurd cried. "I might be dying!"

Steve twisted about in his saddle to look back at Spurd. The outlaw was bound to his own horse, which Steve led. "Doctor?" he echoed. "Who said anything about a doctor?"

He closed his ears to the stream of furious curses that Spurd unleashed, although a number of Guthrie's citizens on the street paused in their activities to stare. At this mid-hour of the summer afternoon, the territorial capital's streets lacked much of the bustle that characterized the morning and evening hours, but there was still a lot of traffic, ranging from horsemen to carriages to pedestrians.

Traveler's shod hooves clattered on bricks which only recently had replaced the dirt on several of Guthrie's main streets. Steve found his eyes drawn as always to the elaborate stonework of the turrets and arched windows adorning many of the buildings. They were the trademark of Joseph Foucart, the eccentric European architect who had settled in Guthrie and ended up designing many of its buildings.

Conceived from its inception as the territorial capital,

the young plains city, boasting electric lights, an elaborate water and sewage system, and a network of underground tunnels connecting various businesses, was a showplace to rival many of the well-established Eastern cities. Steve still marveled at the transformation of what a few short years before had been empty prairie land.

As he reined Traveler to a halt in front of the U.S. marshal's office, he was conscious of the dirt and grit of his days on the trail. He was also conscious of the wearying tension that came of playing captor to a ruthless killer such as Zeke Spurd. Even now, having reached his destination, the tenseness would not quite dissipate.

"I see you got him." Deputy Marshal Heck Thomas had just emerged from his office, apparently having seen Steve's arrival. He stood on the boardwalk, hands on his lean hips, and gazed up at Steve from beneath his Stetson.

Past sixty now, Thomas still served capably as the primary proponent of law and order in the territory. Steve knew that the older man had fought under Stonewall Jackson in the Civil War and, later, as a Texas Ranger, he had brought the notorious Lee Brothers to justice. His far-reaching reputation, coupled with his ability to live up to it, helped to keep the peace in the rowdy young capital.

Steve dismounted and gripped Heck's hand firmly. "I got him," he said. "He was down in the Wichitas, and I had some help—Velador."

Heck's eyebrows rose in surprise. "The Watcher?" he translated the Spanish name. "Is he still around?"

Steve nodded, then explained what had happened in the mountains.

Heck shook his head in wonder. "I ran into him a few times when I was in the Rangers, long before your day," he said. "By gad, he was old even then. There's no telling how long he's been up in those mountains. Nobody seems to know how he came by that name, either."

"Hey, I need a doctor!" Spurd yelled. He emphasized his demand with another curse.

"I patched him up some," Steve said, "but he's probably right."

"Yeah. Well, he'll get everything he needs," Thomas drawled. "I want him in good shape when he hangs." His eyes, as he looked past Steve at Spurd, were like the steel of a .45. The outlaw lapsed abruptly into silence.

Heck looked again at Steve. "Incidentally, if you're interested in heading back to the Wichitas, I volunteered your services as a guide to some Spanish folks who came to town the other day."

"Spanish?" Steve said.

Heck nodded. "The real thing—aristocrats all the way from Spain. Sid Taggar over at the bank is kind of watching over their interests. They wanted a guide, someone who could handle himself and knew his way around those mountains. I gave them your name."

"What's it about?"

"I'm not really sure. Even Sid is awful closemouthed about it all. But I'm sure he wouldn't go along with anything crooked. Anyway, they're awful eager to see you. If it's okay, I'll tell them nine o'clock tomorrow morning over at the Palace Hotel."

Steve shrugged. "Sure. I can always use the money. One of these days I'll have enough saved up to stop trying to build a decent herd out of one bull and a handful of heifers."

"Speaking of which—turn in a statement for your time and I'll see that you're paid. Remember, I can still use another good full-time deputy."

Steve grinned. "No, thanks. I don't mind earning a few bucks along the way as a part-timer when you need one, but I had enough of a career as a lawman in the Rangers."

Heck chuckled. "Suit yourself. But, by gad, you sure haven't lost the touch."

Leaving Spurd to the marshal's mercies, Steve headed Traveler out of town, eager to get back to his spread. He knew he had left it in good hands in the person of Charlie Hallick, whom, though partially crippled, he had taken on as a full-time cowhand over a year before.

It would sure feel good to sleep again in the log cabin he had built after claiming the property in the land run back in '89. To that cabin, which he shared with Charlie, Steve had added a barn and a corral. Despite his gloomy tone with Thomas, he knew he had the makings of a fine herd of beef cattle and the pastureland to support several additional head. With his earnings from his stint as a special deputy to apprehend Zeke Spurd, along with what he had already accumulated from similar ventures, he would be able to add some quality breeding stock to his fledgling herd. And if the job of guide that Heck Thomas had arranged came through, he might have an even larger stake with which to work. He wondered what need the Spanish aristocrats might have for a guide to take them to the Wichita Mountains.

Charlie hobbled out from the barn to greet him as he rode in, and he spent the rest of the afternoon checking on his cattle and going over details with Charlie. As he had expected, everything was in good order. Grateful for Steve's offer of room and board and a modest share of any future profits, Charlie had proved himself trustworthy and capable of minding the place in Steve's absence.

Charlie had heard nothing of any party of Spaniards arriving in town, he told Steve when asked, not having left the spread while Steve was gone. Steve put his musings aside, but they returned to him that evening before he went to bed. So it was with an air of curiosity that he headed Traveler back into Guthrie the following morning. Planning to sweep across his land in search of strays before he returned to the cabin, he had donned clean range garb. He hoped it would be appropriate for the meeting.

The city was busy with its usual morning clamor, and he threaded Traveler past the other riders and vehicles with which he shared the streets. His impatience to learn about his potential employers had gotten him to town in plenty of time for the morning meeting. He could already see the elaborate stone face of the plush Palace Hotel ahead. Almost directly across from it was the more somber front of the Mercantile Bank where Sid Taggar reigned as president.

A recalcitrant mule, balking at the loaded wagon his irate owner urged him to pull, made Steve bring Traveler to a halt in front of the Blue Belle Saloon. Steve glanced at the notorious saloon, noting the covered walkway that connected its second story to the adjacent hotel. Male patrons of the hostelry, he knew, made frequent use of the walkway.

The wagon driver got his mule moving, and Steve urged Traveler forward. He drew him up again as a tall man coming from the direction of the Palace cut in ahead of him. The man swung agilely up onto the boardwalk in front of the bar. Turning, he hooked his right thumb in his tooled gun belt near the low-slung .45 and used his other hand to tilt back the brim of his black Stetson.

"Welcome back, Lawton," he said with a sneer. "I hear you brought in poor old Zeke with a bullet hole in him."

"It was his choice, Joe." Steve held Traveler still and resisted the urge to drop his hand to the butt of his .45. "I always give a man a choice."

"Anybody ever give you a choice, Lawton?" Joe Starr grinned as he said the words, but there was no humor in that baring of his yellowed teeth. He was tall and of average build. The beginnings of a gut strained his gun belt and gave mute evidence of his dissipation. His stance carried a subtle suggestion of menace as he gazed insolently up at Steve.

"I make my own choices," Steve said. He knew that Heck Thomas was awaiting his opportunity to jail Joe Starr or run him and his crew out of Guthrie. But so far, Starr had been careful to give the lawman no cause to roust him, although his reputation as a soldier of fortune, gunman, and sometime range detective made him the object of the marshal's continued scrutiny.

Starr ran at the head of a small pack of equally disreputable rabble, but there was no sign of any of his companions. They spent much of their time at the Blue Belle, and Steve wondered if the others were inside the bar even now.

"You're out early," Steve said.

"Just doing a little bit of business." Starr's grin didn't falter. He wore dark pants and a dark vest over a pale shirt. The clothes, once expensive, were now soiled and shabby. Starr's lean face, like his body, was beginning to bear the marks of his dissipation. There was a puffiness around his eyes, and the beginnings of jowls under his chin.

Steve didn't respond to Starr's answer, but sat his horse, staring flatly at the other man. The old habits rode him, and he did not want to go on and leave his back open to this man, with his threatening stance and low-slung .45.

After a moment Starr's grin faltered slightly. Then he stepped carefully backward, reaching behind him to open the batwing doors of the bar.

"Someday I'll give *you* a choice, Lawton," he said, and then he disappeared into the saloon.

Steve heeled Traveler forward, then let his hand drop to the butt of his Colt reassuringly. He did not look back, although he wondered if Starr watched him from within the saloon.

The bulk of the Palace Hotel loomed up in front of him. He guided Traveler down the ramp into the shaded recess where a couple of carriages were already parked. He tied Traveler to the hitching rail, then went back up the ramp and into the Palace's plush lobby.

He halted inside the door, surveying the room, with its elegant seating arrangements and their occupants. He started to cross to the clerk stationed behind the mahogany desk. Suddenly a stir among a group seated to his left drew his attention.

Three people were rising from matching upholstered chairs. One of them, a man, came forward to greet him, a slightly questioning expression on his thinly handsome face. "Señor Lawton?" he asked.

Steve nodded and gripped the hand the other offered. He met the gaze of intense eyes set in dark patrician features, which, although past middle age, were still lean and handsome. The stranger was clad in what Steve recognized as the elaborate garb of the Spanish upper class. He gave a little bow of acknowledgement as his hand gripped Steve's firmly.

"Permit me to introduce myself." His accented English was excellent. "I am Don Carlos Ruiz Alejandro. If you are indeed Señor Steve Lawton, then I and my companions are the party you are scheduled to meet. Señor Taggar from the bank has, unfortunately, not arrived as yet."

"I'm Steve Lawton. Pleased to meet you."

"And now allow me to introduce my two wards to you." As he spoke, he stepped aside and made a little sweeping gesture to present his two companions.

Steve's eyes were drawn first to the girl. Tumbling black hair framed a face that carried the soft feminine curves of traditional Latin beauty, but which was yet suffused with something more, a kind of compelling warmth. It lent the classic features an alluring loveliness that almost stole Steve's breath away. The modest high-necked dress she wore, with its full skirt and elaborate petticoats, seemed only to emphasize the richness of a figure that might still lack a year of attaining its full blossom. He guessed her age at not over twenty.

"My ward, Señorita Felicia Consuela Vendegas," Alejandro said with a courtly flourish.

Steve doffed his Stetson, took her extended hand in his fingertips, and bowed slightly. He wasn't sure if it was appropriate etiquette, but it seemed to serve. When he tried to catch her gaze, she lowered her eyes modestly and drew back her hand.

"And my other ward, Felicia's brother, Ramon Philipe Vendegas," Alejandro said.

The young man behind Felicia made no effort to step forward and accept Steve's extended hand. The resemblance between him and the girl was obvious, and Steve guessed him to be about two years her junior. His slim form was clad in the tight-fitting dandyish garb of a caballero or a young Latin rake. His delicate features were set in a haughty, supercilious sneer.

"Señor Lawton is the man Marshal Thomas has recommended as our guide," Alejandro said smoothly, ignoring the boy's poor manners.

But the youth was not to be so easily denied. "Him?" His tone was as scornful as the gaze he raked over Steve and his range attire. "He is nothing but a cheap cowhand."

Felicia turned quickly and whispered sharply to her brother in Spanish. Steve saw a flush of embarrassment rise to her pale cheeks. Beneath her scolding and the scathing gaze Alejandro flung at him, Ramon turned angrily away.

"Forgive his manners," Alejandro said to Steve. "He is young and a little hotheaded. He feels he must prove himself here among your Western cowboys."

"Forget it. But if he doesn't wear a gun and know how to use it, he had better watch what he says and who he says it to. Some of our cowboys just might give him a chance to prove himself or die trying."

Ramon apparently heard some of the words, for he turned quickly back. "I can take care of myself, señor. I am not afraid of you or anyone else."

"Good," Steve said coldly. "I hope you never have cause to be."

"Well, I see you've already met," a hearty voice overrode whatever Ramon's response might have been. "My apologies for being late. I had some business I had to tend to. Steve, it's good to see you. I'm glad you could make it."

Although he had met Sid Taggar on only a few other occasions, Steve, for some reason, was being greeted like an old friend by the bank president. Tall, robust, with an outdoorsman's rugged physique and a cat-footed carriage that belied his prominent financial position in the city, Sid

Taggar was a hard man to dislike. Steve found himself responding warmly to the other's greeting.

Taggar was in his thirties, Steve guessed. His curly black hair was beginning to show a few streaks of gray, and his handsome features had a maturity that had not yet given way to the encroachments of age.

He took over the proceedings with the practiced ease of a politician. "I see you're already getting to know one another. Good. Felicia, Ramon, this is the young man I've told your guardian so much about. He knows the Wichita Mountains where you're headed, and he can handle just about any problem you run into. He spent several years as a Texas Ranger before he came up here for the land run."

Ramon's head had jerked up at Taggar's words. "You?" He stared. "A Texas Ranger?"

Steve glanced at a point just above the boy's head and let the remark go by. But he thought he detected the faintest beginnings of a grudging respect in his eyes.

"Well, gentlemen." Taggar seemed to have excluded the brother and sister as he spread open hands toward Steve and Alejandro. "Shall we adjourn to my office? Then we can explain what all this is about to you, Steve."

Steve shrugged, suddenly reluctant to leave the presence of the lovely girl despite her acerbic brother.

Alejandro caught and read his inquiring glance toward the pair. "They will wait here for us." His tone was almost brusque. "I handle all of the Vendegas's business affairs." He turned briefly to his wards. "Stay here. Do not go out. Is that understood, Ramon?"

Ramon's nod was surly. "There is no need to treat us like children. I am quite capable of taking care of my sister and escorting her anywhere she wishes to go."

"Of course, we'll stay here, Carlos," Felicia said, acting as peacemaker between the two Latin males. Steve thought he caught her dark eyes flashing in his direction, but could not be sure.

"Well, that's settled then," Taggar said with hearty cheerfulness. "Let's go over to my office. We won't be long."

Steve allowed himself to be ushered through the door with Alejandro.

Chapter Two

"Let me give you a little bit of background as to how I got involved in all this, Steve," Sid Taggar began. "Then Don Carlos can explain why he and his wards have come here to Guthrie."

Sid Taggar's office was well furnished without being ostentatious. It reflected well the character of a successful businessman who had not forgotten or denied his modest origins. Relaxed behind his massive mahogany desk, Taggar seemed at ease in his element. Steve was seated with Carlos in the heavy upholstered chairs in front of the desk, and Taggar appeared to enjoy having even this small audience.

"When Don Carlos decided to bring his wards here from Spain, he naturally wanted a capable and discreet contact to help him coordinate their business here. He did some checking, and, I'm flattered to say, he then contacted me to serve as his coordinator and agent."

"Señor Taggar's references were of the finest quality," Alejandro said.

Taggar waved the compliment away. "I'm just glad I was able to help. And when Carlos sent word to me of their need for a guide, I, of course, thought of you. I visited with Marshal Thomas and he endorsed my choice."

"Both Marshal Thomas and Señor Taggar have spoken very highly of you," Alejandro told Steve. "And now that I have finally met you, I am pleased with their choice. But you are young to be so experienced."

"Experience isn't always measured in years," Steve said softly.

Alejandro chuckled. "You are right, of course. When I was your age I was well on my way to doubling my family's fortune with investments that other, older and supposedly more knowledgeable, men scorned as too risky. But Señor Taggar tells me you are familiar with the Wichita Mountains, and that in your years as a Ranger and more recently even, you have hunted men there."

"That's right."

"Ah. I have hunted big game in the forests of Europe and the jungles of Africa," Alejandro said. "But I have never hunted men. You shall have to tell me of your experiences." His eyes glittered like ice.

"I'd like to hear more about your interest in the Wichitas."

"Of course. Forgive an avid sportsman his passion." Alejandro seemed to withdraw slightly, the glitter fading from his eyes. "Since you know the Wichitas," he began, "you are undoubtedly aware of Devil's Canyon."

Steve nodded. "I know it. I just got back from there, in fact. I arrested a man in the canyon."

"Excellent! You are certainly the right man for the job."

"Just what is the job?"

Alejandro drew a finger across his neatly trimmed mustache. He cast a glance at the silent Taggar before looking back at Steve. "We are looking for gold in Devil's Canyon," he said. "More precisely, a treasure hidden there for centuries."

Steve laughed. He had not been prepared for the statement, and he regretted his outburst immediately, cutting it off as he saw the intensity in Alejandro's eyes.

"You do not believe that there may be gold in Devil's Canyon?" the don demanded.

"Of course there's gold," Steve told him. "There's even hidden treasure. But which hidden treasure? That left by the mysterious Mexican miners, or the one stolen and buried by the Indians, or those hidden there by outlaws on the run? Take your pick. Why, there are over a dozen tales and legends linking that canyon to lost treasure. But to date, no one that I've heard of has ever succeeded in actually finding any of it."

"They did not know where to look," Don Carlos said. "Yes, there are legends. The story of the gold we seek was the origin of all those tales." His words were almost a challenge.

"Suppose you tell me that story," Steve said matter-of-factly.

"Very well." Alejandro had lost none of his intensity. "But let me start by asking you a question. You are obviously familiar with these mountains and their legends. Tell me, who do you believe were the first Europeans to reach those mountains?"

"Your own people, of course," Steve answered immediately. "Spanish explorers crisscrossed this whole area in the seventeenth and eighteenth centuries."

"Exactly." Alejandro might have been a schoolmaster praising a backward student. "And what do your legends say was the earliest party actually to reach the Wichitas?"

Steve thought carefully. He was familiar with some of

the legends of gold in Devil's Canyon, and had picked up
bits of others over the years. It would be almost impossible
for him to have done otherwise. The remote canyon had
spawned a tangled web of tales, repeated and elaborated
on by lonely men around their campfires at night throughout the territory. Stacks of gleaming gold ingots, so the
stories went, lay buried and forgotten in dark caverns,
guarded by the bones of the dead and perhaps by the devil
himself. They awaited only the searcher with the luck and
skill to find them and claim them as his own.

"Perhaps the party of Father Juan de Salas around
1629," Steve answered Alejandro's question. "Or a certain
Father Gilbert in 1657, who mined the canyon for gold."

Alejandro was shaking his head. "They were not the
first, and Father Gilbert was actually seeking only the
same gold that we are. He never found it, nor has anyone
who came after him."

"But you have a map." Steve could not quite hide the
sarcasm in his voice. Treasure maps for the Wichitas were
almost as common as the treasure tales themselves.

"Yes, we have a map!" Alejandro declared with a fiery
intensity. "One that has passed down from generation to
generation in the Vendegas family, and which was drawn
by a member of that family who actually helped bury the
gold."

"The Vendegas family," Steve said. "That's the girl and
her brother."

Alejandro nodded. He seemed caught up in his explanation now, gripped by a need to divest himself of the burden
of its weight. "Early in the seventeenth century, before
even Juan de Salas visited this area, a party of Spanish
conquistadores led by Captain Ricardo Vendegas came to
the Wichita Mountains in their explorations. Captain

Vendegas was an educated man, and he recognized the potential for gold in those mountains. He and his men sank a mine shaft over one hundred feet deep in what you now call Devil's Canyon. And they were successful in their efforts, so successful in fact that they remained in the canyon for several years, even establishing a small settlement there. And they set up a foundry in a nearby cave, using metal crucibles to melt down the gold and cast it into ingots for eventual transport to Spain."

Steve thought of the brush-choked floor and barren walls of the canyon. Had the old Spanish conquistadores, driven by their greed, actually lived and labored there almost three hundred years ago? He listened intently as Alejandro continued:

"But during their years there, they eventually angered a tribe of Indians who viewed that valley as sacred and who resented the presence of the conquistadores. Finally, in one day of fire and blood, the Indians fell on the conquistadores and slaughtered them, casting their bodies into the mine shaft. Only Captain Vendegas and his second-in-command were spared, perhaps because of their status as leaders. They forced Captain Vendegas and his companion to move the gold ingots that they had worked so long to produce—fifty burro loads in all—to another cave accessible only through a narrow, concealed cleft, and left it there. But they placed markers to indicate the spot—a great stone turtle outside the canyon itself, and carvings of turtles on trees and stone formations in the mountains. The turtle, because of its ability to conceal itself in its shell, was their symbol for that which was hidden. They filled in the shaft."

"What happened to the captain and his lieutenant?" Steve asked, gripped by the story.

"The Indians kept them as slaves." Alejandro might have been gazing back over those centuries to the two adventurers and their desperate plight. "For three years they served the Indians as slaves. Then, at last, they managed to escape, although the captain's companion was wounded. He eventually died of his wounds, leaving Captain Vendegas to travel cross-country on foot. He finally made contact with a small Spanish mission in what is now northern Texas. It was another two years before he was able to return to Spain. His health was ruined by his ordeal, and he never left his homeland again.

"He had recorded the precise location of the gold on a map and in his personal journal. But he was so distressed by his experiences that he made his children swear an oath not to attempt to return and claim the gold. And he made them swear that they would demand the same oath of their children when they reached adulthood, and on down through the generations. Captain Vendegas was convinced that the canyon and its gold belonged to the devil himself, but he could not bear to destroy the map or his journal, believing they might have historical significance to the family someday. So the map has passed down to each succeeding generation of the Vendegas family." Alejandro paused. "There, Señor Lawton. That is the true story of the gold of Devil's Canyon."

Steve sat silently for a time, mulling over the man's words. Alejandro's tale carried a certain plausibility, and it did seem to incorporate fragments and elements of many of the legends and mold them into a whole. He had heard of the mysterious ruins in the canyon although he had never seen them. And an old prospector had once told him of a great turtle, fashioned of stones, that could be found on the prairie at the edge of the mountains. Then, too, he himself had once seen, carved on a stone promontory, the unmistakable outline of a turtle.

"So you've come to find the gold," he said at last. "What happened to the father of Felicia and Ramon?"

"Don Jorge Diego Vendegas, their father, was my dear friend and business associate for many years. His death some six years ago was quite unexpected, and since he was a widower and I had many close ties with his family, I was named guardian of his children and given the legal charge of managing their financial affairs. There are no other surviving members of the Vendegas family except Felicia and Ramon. They are the last of the line, and, unfortunately, the family's wealth has been depleted over the years. A recent series of financial setbacks, involving my own resources as well as those of the Vendegas, has left us in financial straits. Faced with this situation, and with the responsibility and obligation of looking after their interests, I determined to come here to America and recover the hoard of gold, which, by rights, belongs to Felicia and Ramon."

"What about the oath?" Steve asked.

Alejandro waved a hand, dismissing the issue. "A sick old man's foolishness. Surely he would not have desired his descendants to suffer the hardships and ignominies of poverty for the sake of his deluded demands. Besides, they are both yet minors. They are not bound by any oath that would have been requested of them by their father upon adulthood. I knew of the map and of the story of their ancestor and the gold. I would have been sadly remiss in both my legal and my moral obligations to my friend's children if I had not pursued this opportunity."

"Do you actually think you can find the gold after this long?"

The don spread his hands wide. "I have nothing to lose in trying," he said. "And there is no reason why the gold should not still be where it was cached three centuries ago. News of a find like that would have been impossible to keep secret. And you yourself said you were not aware of anyone actually finding hidden gold in Devil's Canyon. It is because no one, except the members of the Vendegas family, have ever had all the precise coordinates for locating the gold. What others have based their searches on are but fragments of the story told by Captain Vendegas at the Texas mission, and they were twisted and distorted by retelling over the years."

Alejandro certainly seemed to believe the story, Steve thought, and there was no good reason why the two surviving Vendegases should not have access to the gold mined by their ancestor. If, of course, the gold actually existed and it could be found.

"A lot can change in three hundred years," he said. "Landslides are common in those mountains, as are flash floods on the rare occasions when it does rain. Wind and natural erosion can change the face of things over that long a period. Even if I take you to the mountains, there's no guarantee we'll find the gold."

"I know that, señor," Alejandro said. "But I also know that I could never rest easily with myself if I had not made the effort."

Steve glanced at Taggar, and the bank president seemed to take that as his cue to rejoin the conversation. "I've seen the map," he said, "and I believe that it's authentic. I think there's a good chance that they can locate the gold. I've agreed to have the bank finance their expedition. I would not have done so had I not believed in their chances."

A treasure hunt hardly seemed like a prudent undertaking for a bank loan, Steve conjectured. But Taggar was well known in Guthrie, and his reputation for integrity and astuteness was beyond question. That a man of his standing was willing to give his wholehearted backing, financial and personal, to the enterprise certainly lent it a solid credibility.

"We're willing to pay you twice the wages you would make working as a special deputy for Marshal Thomas," Taggar continued.

"And, of course, a bonus if we should find the gold," Alejandro added. "Would a thousand dollars be acceptable?"

Steve thought of what he could do for his spread with a thousand dollars. Such a sum would easily allow him to get his ranch to a stage where it could be operated at a profit. Then he banished the thought firmly. He did not for a moment believe that the Spanish aristocrat and his wards would be successful in their venture. He had heard too many tales over the years, seen too many men squander time and money and effort and sometimes even their lives in pursuit of the elusive phantom of buried treasure.

But the wages Taggar offered were good, and he had warned them of their chances. He could do the job in good faith even if they did not find the treasure. "There's no need of a bonus. I work for my wages alone," he said. "I'll take the job, though. But remember, I won't guarantee results. I can take you to those mountains and guide you to Devil's Canyon. Beyond that, it's up to that map of yours."

"That is all we ask," Alejandro assured him. "Your skill as a guide and, if necessary, as a protector. Since Felicia will be accompanying us, I am glad to have a man of your reputation in our employ."

"Hold it a minute," Steve cut in. "You're taking the girl along? Into the Wichitas?"

"But of course," Alejandro said. "The treasure will belong to her and her brother. She has every right to be present when we find it. Further, she insists upon going."

"Maybe Marshal Thomas or Mr. Taggar didn't tell you," Steve said, "but the Wichitas are sanctuary for half the owlhoots and outlaws in the territory. Taking a woman with us, particularly a young, good-looking one, is asking for trouble." But still, he admitted to himself, the idea of having the lovely Felicia along on this expedition was not unappealing.

"There will be four armed men accompanying her," Alejandro countered. "And Felicia herself is an expert with a rifle. I have seen to that myself. She has gone with me on more than one big-game hunt. And so has Ramon."

"Who's the fourth man?" Steve asked, then glanced across the desk at Taggar and knew the answer.

"Even if my bank wasn't providing the financing," Taggar said, "I wouldn't miss this venture for the world. It's been too long since I got out from behind this desk, strapped on a gun, and sat a horse like a man." He grinned at Steve with an engaging warmth.

Steve recalled the stories of Taggar's early years as a cowhand and later as a trail boss on one of the last cattle drives. It was said that the bank president, during those days, had been a man to reckon with in the use of fists and guns. And Taggar did not seem to have lost any of the mental or physical toughness that had been an earmark of his earlier trade.

Taggar, Steve himself, and Alejandro, with his supposed skill as a hunter, would make a formidable group, Steve admitted. Ramon was an unknown quantity, although his performance back at the hotel did not bode well in that regard. But they should still be enough to discourage any but the largest of bands of renegades they might encounter.

Taggar seemed to read his acceptance in his eyes. "It is, of course, vitally important that the reason for our expedition remain a secret," he said. "Only the three of us and Felicia and Ramon know about the map. No one else knows why Don Carlos and the Vendegases are here in Guthrie. And it is essential that we keep it that way."

"Right," Steve agreed. News of a treasure map and a search for lost gold would be sure to bring the fortune seekers and scavengers out from under their rocks. It was the kind of attention that the enterprise could do without.

"I'll need a day or so to get things squared away at my place," he said. "And we'll need to get supplies."

"I'll take care of that," Taggar offered. "You can double-check it all before we leave, if you like."

Steve nodded, then glanced inquiringly at Alejandro.

"We are ready, my friend," the Spaniard answered his unspoken question. "The Vendegas children and I have come all the way from Spain for this undertaking."

"The day after tomorrow, then," Taggar said. "Is eight o'clock that morning all right with everyone?"

Steve nodded, then turned his head toward the door as a young man with the ink-stained fingers of a bookkeeper came hesitantly into the office.

"I told you nothing was to disturb us!" Taggar's voice thundered as if he was back giving orders on the trail drive.

The young man flinched. "I'm sorry, sir, but Señorita Vendegas is here. She seems upset."

Before he could continue, Felicia pushed breathlessly past him into the office. Those exquisite features were pale, her dark eyes wide. *"Con permiso,"* she began hurriedly in Spanish, then switched to English: "Excuse me, but Ramon has left the hotel. I tried to stop him, but he would not listen. He said he was *un hombre* and would do as he pleased. I watched to see where he went, and it was to the cantina, the Blue Belle. He has not come out, and now there is a crowd in front. I am worried that something has happened, that he is in trouble."

That would not be a bad bet, Steve thought. The Blue Belle—hangout of Joe Starr and his cronies. "Come on," he said, rising. "Let's get over there!"

Chapter Three

*T*he crowd in front of the Blue Belle Salon was a shifting, shouting mass of local riffraff and transients mingled with a few farmers eager to see the unexpected excitement. Steve elbowed his way through them. Some of the locals, recognizing him, seeing the expression on his face, drew back to let him pass. He had lost track of Sid Taggar and the others by the time he broke through the front rank of the crowd inside the small saloon.

Felicia Vendegas's instincts had been good. Ramon was in trouble. The saloon consisted of a single room with the bar against the opposite wall. The other walls were lined three deep with shouting, exhorting spectators. Their attention was centered on the cleared area in front of the bar and the two combatants there.

It could not have been much of a combat, however. Ramon Vendegas, his fine caballero's outfit somewhat the worse for wear, was slumped half erect against the bar, his boyishly handsome face bloody. Only his left arm propped on the bar held him erect, and his right hand seemed to be groping down his leg toward his boot. Steve recognized the hulking man towering over Ramon, massive fist uplifted for what would certainly be the finishing, the killing, blow.

"Jackson!" Steve's voice crashed through the uproar of the spectators and arrested that big fist in mid-descent.

The bullet head surmounted by the long, greasy mat of hair swiveled in Steve's direction. "Lawton." The big man exhaled his name in recognition, and a wildness flared in the small, sunken eyes beneath the heavy, scarred brow.

"It's my turn now," Steve said, just loudly enough to be heard.

The big man put his head back and laughed with a brutal glee. Ramon slumped the rest of the way to the floor, obviously barely conscious, right hand still groping feebly at his boot. Ignoring him, his conqueror stepped away from the bar. Even across a distance of six feet, Steve found himself looking up at the brutal face with its scar tissue from countless other barroom and back-alley brawls.

"You looking for a real fight, Bruiser?" Steve asked in a taunting voice. "Or are you just beating up children today?"

Bruiser Jackson's thick lips curled in a kind of grin, revealing the blackened stubs of what few of his front teeth had survived his brawling career. Past one big shoulder Steve saw the sneering face of Joe Starr in the forefront of the ranks of spectators. Steve was not surprised. Bruiser Jackson was one of the thugs who answered to Starr's orders.

Known throughout the territory as a brutal, rough-and-tumble fighter, Bruiser Jackson was the muscle Starr used when fast guns would not accomplish his ends or the ends of his questionable employers. Bruiser was big and broad, and there did not seem to be much fat on him beneath his soiled clothes.

And Ramon had managed, against all odds, to mark the big man, Steve saw. A trickle of blood ran from the corner of Jackson's mouth. Had Bruiser picked the fight with Ramon? Almost certainly that was the case, and, if so, why? Starr and his men usually worked only for pay, although Jackson's savage nature alone might have been enough motivation for him to pick on the foppish young Spaniard. And with Ramon's arrogant mouth, Steve thought grimly, it would not have taken much prodding to begin the action. But Bruiser had been dangerously close to killing his opponent.

A cold determination rose in Steve, and he circled away into the open area to get room as Bruiser came forward, scarred fists lifting. Steve lifted his own fists. Bruiser gave a slobbering snort of derision and came at him in a bull-like rush, clubbed right fist coming around in a swing that could easily break a man's neck. Instinctively, Steve ducked inside that sweeping arm, hooking his own right into Bruiser's middle. He felt his fist meet hard, unyielding flesh, and then Bruiser's massive body rammed into him, driving him back like he was a child. Bruiser's first blow had been little more than a ruse, he realized, intended only to set him up for the rushing impact of Bruiser's bulky body, which bid fair to drive the air from his lungs.

Bruiser's left fist slammed agonizingly into his side even as he stumbled back before the big man's rush. Then his shoulders came up hard against the wall, the spectators having scattered out of his path. Bruiser was looming over him, one huge fist uplifted like a hammer to crash down on the side of his neck. Desperately, Steve wrenched himself aside, and the descending fist glanced off his shoulder like a blacksmith's hammer. He was still virtually pinned against the wall, and fear clawed in him at the thought of taking many more of Bruiser's blows.

But he was inside the bigger man's guard, and Bruiser had lurched off balance from his missed hammer blow. Steve set himself and hooked right and left into the midriff again, getting his shoulders into the blows, and this time feeling some give in the meaty flesh beneath his fists. Bruiser's breath, hot and foul, belched into his face. He hooked left and right again, head down, elbows working, getting into a rhythm. Bruiser was big and strong, but not even he could withstand that pounding to his middle.

The big man went back an involuntary step, and Steve's fist came from down low, traveling up in an uppercut that intercepted Bruiser's jaw and snapped his bullet head back. Steve sidestepped to get clear. He had done enough damage in close, and he wanted to get out of range of those mallet fists. But it was Bruiser's open hands that shot out and clamped on his face and head, the thick blunt fingers biting in like pliers, stifling breath and vision.

Steve felt his head being twisted around, fiery lightning stabbing into his spine. He knew that his neck was being flexed, that Bruiser was all but lifting him from the floor, rotating his head around in an awesome display of strength that, in only moments, would break his neck. His arms flailed futilely against Bruiser's bulk. He had a distorted view of the crowd, of Joe Starr's leering face, of Bruiser's head flung back as he exerted all the massive strength of his arms and torso to wring Steve's neck.

As red flame clouded his vision, Steve focused on that straining column of Bruiser's neck and lashed his right fist awkwardly around into the vulnerable throat. Bruiser's contorted mouth gaped wide suddenly, and his awful grip loosened fractionally. Steve struck again at the throat, more solidly this time, then again as Bruiser's jaw lowered reflexively to protect that vital spot. With a wrenching heave Bruiser flung him away, one big hand flying to his battered throat.

Steve caught his balance. There was no time to think of how near he had been to death, of the red-hot spike that seemed to have been driven between the vertebrae of his neck. Bruiser was pawing at his throat, croaking in baffled outrage. Steve's back was to the bar now. He stepped in and hit Bruiser's temple, a hard driving right, trying to finish this while he was still able.

Bruiser stumbled, but then, as Steve swung again, his brawling reflexes took over. He ducked his head, hunching his huge shoulders. Steve's blow glanced off the greasy mat of hair atop his head. Before Steve could strike again, Bruiser lunged as he had at the beginning of the fight, right fist looping out to set his smaller opponent up for the bruising impact of his massive body behind it.

Steve saw the tactic and recognized it. He bent low as Bruiser came, shoving his arm between those tree-trunk legs, twisting his torso to take that lunging weight on his shoulders. Then he straightened in one upward, thrusting convulsion of effort that used Bruiser's own momentum to lift him up from the floor and heave him over Steve's head to crash down flat on his back on the bar with an impact that seemed to shake the building.

Bruiser's own bulk made the fall devastating, left him sprawled, winded and half senseless, atop the bar, head hanging at Steve's side. Steve was already turning, not as fast as he would have liked, but fast enough. As he turned, he wrapped his left hand around his right fist, lifting his clenched hands overhead. He swayed a moment, then caught himself and brought that double fist down with all his might into Bruiser's uplifted face. The impact banged the greasy head solidly off the front of the bar, and the angry light still flickering in the sunken eyes went out. Steve dumped his senseless form the rest of the way to the floor.

The spectators, he realized dimly, had gone silent. He glimpsed wide eyes, expressions of awe and disbelief. He looked down at the huge man at his feet. It seemed he could still feel those steel fingers twisting his neck. It had been a close thing. Another few moments and Bruiser's huge hands would have broken his neck as surely as any hangman's noose.

Farther down the bar Ramon was coming unsteadily to his feet. His eyes, too, were fixed on Steve, and Steve guessed that the young Spaniard had witnessed much of the fight.

Steve stepped toward him, taking his arm. "Are you all right?" he asked. Up close, he could see that the damage inflicted by Bruiser, although undoubtedly painful, was not permanent.

Ramon nodded breathlessly in response to the question. Then his eyes focused behind Steve, and his arm went tense in Steve's grasp.

Steve pivoted on the balls of his feet. Joe Starr had stepped forward from the ranks of the spectators, his sneer still in place. Behind him two slender men, clad alike in pale buckskins, had also edged out of the crowd. Steve's hand dropped reflexively to hang near his holstered .45 as he saw them.

Starr noted the movement and chuckled harshly. "Why, you know Simon and Luther Meade, don't you?"

he said expansively, and stepped aside as he spoke, leaving a clear corridor between Steve and the two men.

"I know them," Steve said tightly. He did not look again at Starr. The real danger now was in these two slender young men. Simon and Luther Meade were identical twins, and even though he had seen them before, the similarity between them now tapped icy fingers on the nape of Steve's neck. Curly blond hair topped delicate, feminine features from which gazed cruel, empty eyes. The only difference between them was the pearl-handled .45's they wore slung low at their sides. Simon's was on his left, Luther's on his right. They stood side by side, facing Steve so that their gun hands were on the outside. Their loose stances, their almost winsome expressions, might have been mirror images.

Those fancy guns were not for show, Steve knew. These two, working for Joe Starr, had established a deadly reputation throughout the territory with those .45's. Facing them, still weak from his brutal clash with Bruiser, Steve was extremely aware that he was in no shape to find out if the bizarre pair lived up to their reputation.

"You're pretty good with your hands, Lawton," Starr said. "I didn't think you could take Bruiser."

"You ought to keep him on a chain," Steve said. He still did not look at Starr. He knew this confrontation was not finished yet.

"Of course, I always hate to see one of my boys get whipped," Starr continued amicably. "It hurts my reputation as well as his, if you know what I mean. It makes it harder to get work."

"You don't have much of a reputation to be proud of, Starr."

Again the rasping chuckle. "That's good coming from an ex-Ranger who's still supposed to be one of the best."

"That's finished now."

"Is it really? Zeke Spurd might say different. He was a friend of mine. You know that, Lawton?"

"It figures."

"Simon and Luther here are proud of their reputation, just like I am. You know the story behind them, don't you?"

"Just working for you says enough." Steve's strength was rapidly returning. He was conscious of Ramon hovering at his back, but the youngster was unarmed and, with his lack of experience, would be only a hindrance in what was to come. And against the Meade twins, he could expect no help from any of the spectators.

"Well, now everybody knows Simon and Luther are twins, that they always work together," Starr said. "But there's not many folks who know that they were actually joined together at birth, arm to arm and hand to hand, Simon's right to Luther's left. The doctor had to separate them, and to this day neither of them can use those hands quite like normal. I even talked to an old Indian medicine man once, and he told me that twins being joined like that was real bad medicine. It means the twins are really one person—they think alike, act alike. Why, each one even knows what the other's thinking. Now, I don't know if I believe all that, but having had more than one occasion to see these boys in action, I sure wouldn't bet against it being true."

A feral light seemed to have illuminated the near-angelic faces of the twins. Steve could detect a subtle tension gathering itself in those slender bodies beneath their relaxed postures.

"Like I said, Simon and Luther are mighty proud of their reputation," Starr went on. "And they've earned it, I can tell you. And they've gotten so good now that there's hardly anybody in the territory who might have a chance against them. That is, except you."

"Don't make me kill them, Starr," Steve said evenly.

Starr's chuckle was like a file grating on stone. "But they want to try you, Lawton. They've heard how good you are, and they want to see if they're better. And personally I'd kind of like to see, myself. Besides, you whipped Bruiser, and that makes us all look bad. The way I see things, it's up to the twins here to redeem us."

"You're a long way from redemption." Steve concentrated on the twins, focusing himself on them, seeing their hands brush together almost as if still joined. His palm felt the pull of the .45 at his waist.

"Call them off, Starr."

The voice was not loud, but somehow it made the twins' blissful smiles falter, and it stilled Starr's next words.

Steve allowed himself a single peripheral glance, and saw with relief that Deputy Marshal Heck Thomas had dealt himself a hand in the game. The aging lawman stood just inside the saloon doors in an opening the spectators had made for him. But there was nothing of age or uncertainty in his easy stance, as casual as that of the twins. He was pointing a sawed-off double-barreled Greener shotgun at Starr and the twins.

"If they try it, Starr, I'll blow them to pieces with the first barrel and you with the second," Thomas spoke again. "Lawton won't even have to lift a hand. Now tell them to back off!"

Starr gave a little nod, and that unholy radiance faded

from the twins' faces. They stepped back, drawing a little bit apart. Neither of them had spoken a word.

Heck came forward, using the shotgun to gesture Starr closer to his pet killers. "I want you and your whole crew out of town, Starr," he drawled casually. "I don't rightly know whether it's legal for me to do that, but I reckon this Greener is as much law as I need right now. But if you disagree, we can always let a judge decide. Of course, you'll all be dead by then, so I don't guess it will matter to you, anyhow."

For once Starr had little to say. He gestured angrily, and two hard cases came forward to help Bruiser to his feet. The whole party, including the twins, edged deject-edly out of the saloon. Starr, the last to go, cast a final, challenging look back at Steve. For a moment he seemed about to speak, then he simply sneered and shouldered through the doors.

Steve forced his muscles to relax, only vaguely aware of the immediate uproar that erupted. Within a moment he found himself the center of a congratulating, backslap-ping mass of men. Heck Thomas pushed his way to him.

"Thanks," Steve said.

Thomas shook his graying head in dismissal. Behind the lawman, Steve saw Sid Taggar and Don Carlos Alejandro. Felicia, her lovely face still pale, had somehow appeared to fuss over Ramon, who was motioning her away as he stared past her at Steve.

"Let them out of here, folks." Heck's voice made the mass of onlookers shift to open a passage to the door.

Felicia turned sharply away from Ramon, irritation fading to concern as her eyes fell on Steve. Abruptly he was aware of the throbbing in his nearly wrung neck, and an unaccustomed weakness in his legs made him falter.

Felicia moved quickly, catching his arm to support him. As they left the saloon, it was not the congratulations of Alejandro or Taggar that Steve was most conscious of. Rather, it was the small pair of firm, warm hands gripping his arm in support.

Chapter Four

"She's a wild town." Sid Taggar glanced back in the direction of Guthrie, then turned his disarming grin on Steve. "Like a wild filly kicking up her heels."

"Sometimes she kicks a little too high and a little too hard," Steve said ruefully, and lifted a hand to massage his neck yet again. He suspected it would be some time before he no longer felt the aftereffects of his brawl with Bruiser.

Taggar laughed heartily and clapped him on his shoulder. The banker sat his big bay gelding with an ease that bespoke his earlier days as a trail boss. He had spurred his mount forward to ride beside Steve as their party left the outskirts of Guthrie and rode out on the open plains.

"I can understand your feeling that way," Taggar said. "But on the whole, there are good people here in the territory, despite the riffraff like Starr and his cronies. Good people willing to stake their claims and challenge a new frontier for better or for worse. Salt of the earth, that's what they are."

"You sound like a politician," Steve said.

Taggar laughed again. "And what's wrong with that?

45

I can think of worse things than being governor of a new state."

They had ridden out of Guthrie while there was still a trace of the morning's coolness. But even that had quickly dissipated, and only the near-perpetual breeze rippling across the prairie offered any relief from the growing heat.

Steve twisted around on Traveler to check the other members of the expedition. He had been thankful to see that all of them had chosen sensible trail garb, and now he saw that all of them were nearly as at ease in the saddle as was Taggar.

Alejandro rode a big-boned sorrel and wore what was probably the proper attire for hunting big game in the forests of Europe. The loose pants and shirt lent themselves well to the American West, Steve thought. Only the don's sporting cap was inadequate in shading the back of his neck from the relentless sun. A handgun rode in a closed holster at his waist, and the elaborately tooled butt of a heavy caliber big-game rifle protruded from his saddle sheath. Steve had examined both weapons before leaving Guthrie. The handgun was of foreign manufacture, one of the few Steve had ever seen. The rifle was a beautiful weapon of a caliber to match Zeke Spurd's Sharps, but with nowhere near its awkward length or weight. It would have dropped a bull buffalo in its tracks had those great beasts still roamed the plains as in years past.

Alejandro met Steve's glance and grinned slightly, lifting his head, like one sportsman acknowledging another as they rode out to the hunt. Steve nodded back, keeping his face expressionless, then let his eyes sweep over the Vendegas sister and brother.

In a dark riding skirt and loose blouse, Felicia smiled

at him, and he found himself returning the smile. Her dark hair was pulled back, and she wore a black, flat-brimmed hat that was more sensible in the sun than her guardian's. She let her eyes drop from Steve's although a smile still played on her full lips. Steve remembered the warmth of her hands on his arm after his fight with Bruiser.

He looked past her at the last member of their party. Ramon's face still bore the marks of the beating he had received, and he rode with his head down, his mouth set in what was almost a pout. Following the fight, he had managed a brief thanks to Steve before lapsing into a sullen moodiness that had yet to leave him.

Alejandro had given Ramon responsibility for the two pack mules, which, attached by a lead rope, trailed behind his horse. Like his sister, he carried a saddle gun—a Winchester. Steve recalled Alejandro's claim that both of them knew how to use a rifle. He hoped he would not have occasion to find out if the claims were true.

"Statehood is coming, you know." Sid Taggar's voice drew Steve's attention back to the banker. "And there will be all sorts of opportunities then for a man who's willing to go after what he wants, and has the money to back his play."

"Meaning yourself?"

"Why not? I've never been afraid to take chances, to reach for what I want. How else do you think a trail drover ended up as a bank president?"

"I never really thought about it," Steve said mildly.

Taggar took no offense. Indeed, he seemed pleased by the remark. "Well, *I* thought about it, and plenty when I was making my moves. When I saw opportunity, I took it, and I never stopped taking it. I'm thinking now about

just what a man would need to get himself elected governor once Oklahoma becomes a state."

"Votes," Steve suggested.

Taggar laughed. "That's right. But, more important, a
man needs money, because one way or another votes can
always be bought."

"Mine's not for sale."

"Of course not!" Taggar agreed. "Not directly, anyway.
But a voter, any voter, will respond to the man who makes
himself known and lets his ideas be known, particularly
when those ideas are good for the territory as well as the
voter."

"Did I just hear a campaign speech?" Steve asked. It
was really quite easy to picture the handsome banker running for political office—and winning.

"No campaign speech," Taggar said. "I'm just making
a point. Running a good campaign takes financial backing,
and I'll have that too."

"The banking business is doing all right, then?"

"In this economy? You bet! Guthrie's booming right
now. Why, a bank couldn't have better conditions to
thrive."

Steve swept his eyes across the rolling prairie. They had
left the road at the edge of town to head out across the
grassland. But this close in, there was still considerable
traffic visible in the distance—horsemen, singly or in
groups, coming or going to town, the occasional wagon
or carriage. He squinted against the sunlight, old habits
making him study any riders or vehicles that came within
a quarter of a mile of them. But he saw nothing to alarm
him, and he told himself he was probably just being foolish. There was no reason anyone should offer hostility to
them. The map was a closely kept secret, and Joe Starr,

while he might bear a grudge, was not likely to risk himself or his men against this many guns unless there was something more in it for him than simple revenge.

"Do you see something, señor?"

Steve had let Traveler drift a little out from the others as he scanned the plains, and he looked around now to see that Felicia had fallen in beside him.

"Nothing of importance," he told her. "And call me Steve, please."

"All right, Steve." She caught his eyes with hers almost in passing, then looked beyond him, squinting a little bit beneath the brim of her hat. "Who are those riders?"

Steve did not want to look away from her face, but he looked where she pointed. "Cowboys from one of the bigger spreads," he said. "They're headed into town. Probably have the day off." Her look conveyed interest, and he pointed to a lumbering covered wagon silhouetted against the sky. "And that's more than likely a drummer headed in."

"A drummer?"

"A traveling salesman," he explained. "He'll have everything on that wagon from firearms for the men to fabrics for the ladies."

"How can you tell from here?"

"See the sunlight reflecting off the wagon there? That's likely from a line of pots and pans he's got strung outside the wagon. It saves him some room and lets him do a little advertising of his wares to boot."

"And those." She pointed, seemingly enjoying the game. "Are they more cowboys?"

Steve followed the direction of her finger. "Yep. You've got good eyes."

She smiled as if pleased with her accomplishment, or

maybe with his rough compliment. Then she sobered.
"That is good. When I saw you looking so stern and grim
at everybody we passed, I thought. . . ."

"You thought what?" Steve prompted.

"That we might be in danger. Those men in Guthrie—
the one that you fought, and his *patron,* and the twins."
She shuddered. "I thought you might be looking for them
to come after us."

Steve shook his head, a little surprised at her percep-
tion. "Just an old habit," he explained. "This is still pretty
much wild country, not so different from what it was when
Guthrie was just a collection of tents. The territory isn't
really civilized yet by any means. But I don't think Joe
Starr would risk his men against our guns just because I
beat his man in a fight. He and his crew will fight, but usually only for money."

She shuddered again, and he thought that she drew a
little closer to him as they rode. He liked the feeling. "And
we're still close to town," he went on. "Heck Thomas has
quite a reputation in these parts, and there are not many
who'd want to risk drawing his attention by pulling a job
so close to his office. But when we reach the Wichitas, it'll
be a different story. Then we'll have to be on guard."

"The mountains are dangerous?"

The sound of her voice, the slight hesitancy with which
she handled the English language, was pleasing to his ears.
He wanted her to speak again, regardless of her words.
"The mountains and the men in them," he replied. "The
terrain is rough, and you have to be careful of landslides
and rattlesnakes and heatstroke once you get in the canyons. There are lots of stories of men going into the Wichitas and never being seen again. But the real danger is from
the men who live in the mountains."

"What men are those?"

He shrugged. "Owlhoots, outlaws, renegades. There are a thousand hiding places in those mountains, and it takes an expert to track someone down once he's made it into them. It's been like that for years. But now that we've got some semblance of civilization in the territory, it has gotten even worse, because more and more hard cases on the run are ending up in those mountains."

"Señor Taggar said that you were once a Ranger in Texas and that you had tracked men in the mountains."

Steve shifted uncomfortably in the saddle. "Some, yeah," he said.

"Is that how you learned to fight? In the Rangers, I mean?"

She was still studying him intently, and he could not tell if it was interest or distaste that he read in her features. Perhaps both. "In the Rangers and other places," he said. "Mostly I learned because I had to to stay alive."

"I saw you fight the man in the saloon. He was so big, so strong. When he grabbed you like that, by the head, I thought that he would kill you."

"So did I," Steve admitted, and her sudden smile was warm with approval. He realized with faint surprise that her good favor was very important to him.

"And Indians?" she asked. "I have read about them and even saw some once in a—how do you say it?—wild West show that came to Spain when I was younger. My father took Ramon and me." Her face clouded for an instant, but she went quickly on: "And I even saw some in Guthrie, but they dressed and acted hardly different from anyone else. Are there Indians in the mountains?"

"Most of the Indians are on reservations now," he told her. "Not too many still live in the mountains." He had an image of the ancient features and gnarled, crippled body of Velador. "And some of them that do are good men," he added.

Steve turned his head and looked to the north. She followed his gaze, then giggled slightly. "What do you see? I cannot see anything."

Steve grinned a little at her teasing. "My place is back over there a little ways. We're not too far from the boundary here."

"Your place?" she asked.

"My home, my spread."

She nodded solemnly, but he thought mischief danced in her dark eyes. "And is it a big spread—*muy grande*—like the ones you said the cowboys came from?"

"No," he said. "Maybe one day. But for now it's just a quarter section—one hundred sixty acres—with a few head of good cattle and enough pasture to support a good number more. But it's home."

"And you will miss it while we are gone?"

"A little," he admitted. "I've got a cabin built, and a barn, and a corral. I'll get more cattle soon. There's a creek that runs through the land, with plenty of trees along it so that the cattle won't hurt for water or shade."

"It sounds wonderful," she said, gazing off to the north as if she could actually see the land and his cabin.

"It is," he assured her. "Maybe you can see it when we get back."

Her eyes came back to his face and met his gaze. "I would like that very much," she said quickly, then lowered her eyes as if embarrassed at her response.

"If you'll excuse me, Felicia dear, I would like to discuss some matters of importance with Señor Lawton." Alejandro had urged his horse up close as he spoke, and

Steve kneed Traveler to the side as the Spaniard pushed his animal between Steve and the girl.

"Certainly," Felicia replied obediently, and she let her horse fall back near Ramon's. Steve was unable to catch her gaze again. He looked over at Alejandro. The Spaniard grinned and drew a finger along his mustache. In his dark eyes, Steve detected the same glitter he had seen back in Taggar's office in Guthrie.

Alejandro said, "Now that we are out here in the wilderness, so to speak, what sort of big game might we encounter?" He lowered a hand to caress the silver inlaid butt of his heavy rifle. "I am eager to try this against your American species."

"Prairie chickens," Steve answered. "Maybe some prairie dogs if we're lucky." Was this one of the matters of importance that Alejandro had wanted to discuss?

"No, I am serious, Stephen. Are there still buffalo on these plains? Antelope, perhaps? What about mountain lions? Wolves? Bears?"

"Let's get one thing settled," Steve said flatly, hearing the irritation in his own voice. "I won't allow any hunting except for food, and then only if our supplies run low. Understand me?"

"No, I do not," Alejandro answered quite seriously. "You are a hunter. I can see it in your eyes, in the way you carry your weapons. You cannot deny it."

"I hunt only when it's necessary."

Alejandro smiled disarmingly. "But surely a man—a hunter—such as you understands that a man must establish his manhood. What is more necessary than that? And the hunt—the stalk, the pitting of oneself against the prey, and finally the kill—is one of the few ways left in which a man may prove himself a man."

"I ran out of things to prove a long time ago," Steve told him. "You mentioned the buffalo. Unnecessary hunting has all but wiped them off the face of the prairie. Within a hundred years there might not be any wildlife left at all. No, Carlos, there are other ways for a man to prove himself."

"Such as going against another man?" Alejandro challenged. "Such as the prisoner you brought in, or the two *pistoleros* at the saloon?" He glanced back in the direction of Felicia, then returned his gaze to Steve.

"Only a fool goes against another man's gun unless he has to," Steve said.

For another moment that glitter danced like sparks in the Spaniard's eyes. Then he laughed pleasantly and slapped the butt of his rifle. "Ah, my friend, you miss some good sport with your gentle ways."

Steve shook his head and urged Traveler once more to the front of the column.

Chapter Five

"**S**eñor, may I speak with you a moment, *por favor?*"

Steve swept the blanket one more time along Traveler's muscled withers, completing his rubdown of the stallion. He looked around at Ramon, who had approached him here at the edge of their first night's camp. They were in a wooded grove that flanked a creek.

"Sure, Ramon," he answered. "What's on your mind? And call me Steve."

Ramon's grin, still a little hesitant, was open and friendly. Steve warmed to the young man. He tossed the saddle blanket over with the rest of his tack equipment and faced Ramon. Behind him he could see their small camp—the tent erected for Felicia's privacy, the cook fire where she tended a skillet, and, on the far side, Taggar and Alejandro sharing a bottle of Kentucky bourbon, which Taggar had produced with a flourish from his saddlebags. Steve had declined the offered drink and started his daily rubdown of Traveler while daylight still remained. Nightfall came late during the summer months. Ramon, he realized, must have likewise declined to join the older men in their drinking.

"I want to apologize, señor—Steve, I mean—for my behavior. And to thank you again for saving my life in the saloon."

The words had not come easily to the young man, but they were sincere. *"De nada,"* Steve murmured. "You were in trouble. I helped you out, that's all."

"No, Steve, you saved my life. The big man would have killed me. I know that, but I have been ashamed, embarrassed, to admit it and to thank you for what you did. It was not until Felicia spoke to me this afternoon that I would admit to myself the debt that I owed you. She said you were a good man and that I dishonored myself as well as her and our family name by behaving as I did."

Steve looked toward where Felicia knelt by the fire, busy in her preparation of their meal. She did not look up, but her head moved slightly, as if she was aware of his gaze and of Ramon's presence with him. "Just what happened in the saloon before I came in?" Steve asked Ramon.

Ramon hesitated briefly, shifting his weight in apparent discomfort. "I left Felicia at the hotel," he began at last. "I wanted a drink and I had seen the saloon. When I had my drink, I saw the big man at a table talking to his *patron*—the one who tried to make you fight the twin *pistoleros.*"

"Joe Starr," Steve supplied.

"Yes." Ramon nodded. "Then the big man got up from the table and came over to me. He asked who I was, and when I told him, he said that he had heard that some foreign greasers were in town. And then he said some things about Felicia that no man should allow another to say about his sister. I had no choice, Steve. I had to hit him."

"Maybe you didn't have a choice then, but you had one when you decided to go into that saloon against Don Carlos's orders," he told him. "You didn't deserve to get killed, but you deserved to run into trouble because that's what you were doing by going into the saloon—looking for trouble." Ramon's lips had thinned, but he stood silent as Steve continued, "One thing you need to know is that when you do go looking for trouble, eventually you're going to find more than you can handle. It just happened to you sooner rather than later. By the grace of God, you're not dead now."

Ramon bowed his head slightly. *"Sí,"* he said after a moment. "I know this. I will not be so stupid again."

Steve looked again at Felicia and imagined that she had lowered her head back to her work just before his eyes fell on her. "You marked him, anyway," he said to Ramon. "Lots of men have been whipped by Bruiser without ever doing that much."

Ramon looked up and smiled at the compliment. "That was my first blow." His features darkened. "After that I could not hurt him, and he seemed to enjoy what he was doing to me. I do not think he wanted the fight to end very soon." He shook his head. "I had not fought like that with my hands, although I knew that is how it is done here. In Spain such matters of honor are settled with *la espada*—the sword. I have trained with a sword before, Steve. And with this." His hand swept down to his boot, and Steve stared at the seven inches of gleaming steel that he withdrew. "Here, Steve." Ramon offered the blade to him, hilt first.

It was a throwing knife, perfectly balanced, its elongated leaf-shaped blade honed to a fine cutting edge on both sides. Steve hefted the weapon a moment, then passed it back to Ramon.

The younger man grinned. "I was not helpless, Steve.

When I realized he meant to kill me, I tried to reach my knife, but then it was too late."

"Can you use it?" Steve nodded at the blade.

Ramon's grin grew even broader. With no warning, his arm swept back and then forward. A gleam of light seemed to leave his hand and spin across twenty feet to bury itself in the trunk of an elm.

Ramon's grin was one of triumph. He went past Steve to retrieve the knife, having to tug hard to pull it free from the trunk. A good two inches of the blade had been embedded in the wood.

Ramon came stalking back, grin still in place. He nodded at the hilt of the bowie sheathed for a cross draw at Steve's waist. "You carry a knife too. But it is not for throwing. It is more like a short sword."

Wordlessly Steve withdrew the huge blade and saw Ramon's eyes widen as its gleaming length was revealed. Steve offered it to him, and he took it, gingerly at first, then more firmly, gripping it, hefting it thoughtfully. His arm went back to throw, and then he lowered it and shook his head. "It is no good for throwing," Ramon declared. "It is too heavy and the balance is wrong." He handed it to Steve, who slid it back into his sheath.

Now Ramon indicated the Colt at Steve's side. "I heard them say you were good with your gun, maybe better than the twin *pistoleros*. And I know you can fight with your hands. Could you teach me, Steve, how to fight with a gun like that and with my hands?"

"I might," Steve said, "but there are more important things to learn. The first lesson is this: No matter how good you are with your knife or a gun or your hands, there's always somebody, somewhere, who's better, or who is going to manage to do something like put a bullet in you while you're trying to pull your knife, or slip a blade between your ribs while you're trying to take a swing at him. No matter how good you are, there's always somebody who can beat you."

And as he said the last word, Steve pulled out the big bowie. As his arm blurred forward, the heavy knife cartwheeled across space to embed itself in the trunk of the elm with an impact that shook it. The point of the blade completely obliterated the scar of white wood that marked Ramon's earlier target.

Ramon stared with wide eyes, his mouth gaping.

"First lesson," Steve said. He went to retrieve the knife.

"I will remember," Ramon told him as he returned.

Steve nodded. "We'll see about the rest later," he promised, then went over to where Felicia was completing the preparations for dinner.

She had fried large pieces of cured ham and then made biscuits and beans. Taggar added a generous dollop of the dwindling bourbon to his coffee and to Alejandro's once the meal was over. He lifted the bottle in Steve's direction. "You thirsty yet, Steve?"

"No, thanks." Steve sipped his coffee. He was aware of the eyes of both Ramon and Felicia on him.

"Not a drinking man are you?" The bourbon seemed to make Taggar even more genial and expressive. Alejandro, on the other hand, had grown silent and pensive, gazing at Felicia and her brother with hooded eyes.

"Haven't you had enough for tonight?" Steve said to Taggar. "We've got another long day in the heat ahead of us tomorrow."

"I believe you are right, my friend." Taggar grinned as he replaced the cork in the bottle. "You have wisdom beyond your years. But I've learned that a few shots of this in the evenings make the nights go a little easier. Do you agree, Carlos, *mi amigo?*"

Alejandro's gaze seemed to linger on Felicia before he looked at Steve. Then he rose wordlessly and crossed to his bedroll. Seating himself, he drew the hunting rifle from its embroidered sheath and began to clean it. In the gathering darkness the firelight glittered on the silver inlays in the weapon's stock.

Taggar grinned at Steve and then got to his feet, took the bottle back to his own bedroll, and replaced it in his saddlebag. Watching him as he undid his bedroll and stretched out on it, Steve noted that despite the bourbon Taggar still moved with a steady efficiency.

Ramon, too, drifted away from the fire. Producing a whetstone, he began honing the twin edges of his throwing knife. Its reflections shifted across the camp as he turned the blade back and forth as he worked.

Steve looked across the low flame at Felicia, who had begun to clean up. She seemed to sense his eyes on her, and she gave him a shy smile, bewitching in the dim light, before returning to her chores.

"The meal was good," Steve told her.

She gave him another quick smile and a murmured acknowledgement. The flames made highlights sparkle like flashing diamonds in her lustrous black hair.

Steve got up and rounded the fire, kneeling beside her where she scoured the skillet with water and sand from the creek. Steve began to repack the provisions that she had used to prepare the meal.

She tossed her hair back in a fetching movement as she turned her head to watch him. "You should not do that," she protested softly. "It is not a man's work."

"I'm used to solitary camps." Steve kept on with his

chore. "If I had to wait for a woman to clean up things in camp or at home, it wouldn't get done."

"Are you lonely when you are by yourself on the prairie?"

"Not only then," Steve answered. He turned his head to see her expression, but she looked back to her work and he could read nothing in the fine lines of her profile.

Neither of them spoke then until the cleaning up had been completed. "Sit down and rest," she told him firmly. "You've done enough. Here, let me take that." Her warm hand brushed against his fingertips as she took the small bundle of provisions from him and placed it with the other supplies. Steve watched the flowing grace of her body as she moved.

He shifted to settle himself more comfortably, and a sharp twinge reminded him of his sore neck. He rubbed at it tiredly.

"Your neck is still hurting?" Turning from the supplies, Felicia had seen his movement.

"A little," he admitted.

"Hold still," she said and came to kneel behind him. In a moment he felt her fingers, strong and firm, begin to massage the back of his neck, probing into his muscles with a soothing, gentle pressure. He let himself relax beneath her touch.

"He hurt you," she murmured. "There are bruises where he held you. Is it better now?"

"Yes," Steve told her. He felt her fingers shift to his shoulders, working there with the same sure pressure and drawing the tension from him. He became extremely aware of her nearness there at his back, the brief touch of her body to his, the faint sweet smell of flowers from some scent she wore.

"When I was a little girl, I used to do this for my father when he was tired." Her voice might have faltered just a little, and the pressure of her fingers lessened for an instant. "He was a big man too," she went on. "And strong like you."

"Felicia dear, I need to talk with Stephen."

Steve turned his head sharply enough to renew the angry twinge in his neck as he felt Felicia's fingers draw away. With the hunting rifle cradled in his arms across his broad chest, Alejandro had come to stand loomingly over them. His handsome, aristocratic features were unreadable in the faint firelight.

"Of course, Carlos," Felicia responded with her customary obedience. "I must get ready for bed. Good night, Steve."

"Good night," he answered her as she disappeared into her tent. He turned his gaze up to Alejandro, who sank easily to his haunches, rifle still cradled in his arms.

"She is a sweet and virtuous girl," Alejandro said. "This country is new to her, exciting. I would not like anyone here to take advantage of her innocence and her excitement."

"My intentions are strictly honorable, Don Carlos," Steve answered with formal seriousness. "Neither you nor she has anything to fear at my hands. I apologize if my actions or my words have been improper. I meant no disrespect."

Alejandro seemed to read the sincerity in his words. He relaxed slightly, settling into a cross-legged position although he kept the big rifle held at port, careful not to let its butt touch the ground. "Perhaps I should apologize," he said, "but I take my duties as her guardian seriously, possibly more seriously than is needed. She is a beautiful girl, but still young and headstrong. It will pass in time, I think, but until then she is my responsibility."

Or until she becomes an adult, Steve thought, but did not speak the words aloud. Alejandro did take his duties seriously. Steve supposed he should respect the man for that.

"I do need to speak with you, Stephen."

"Go ahead," Steve said.

"I could not avoid overhearing some of what you said to Felicia this morning. Is it true that, once in the mountains, there is likely to be danger from the *bandidos* who hide out there?"

"It's possible," Steve said. "Although I wouldn't necessarily say it was likely. We're a well-armed party and we're not greenhorns. That much will be obvious to anyone who sees us. And they would have no reason to know why we are in the mountains."

"That is true. No one knows of the map except those of us who are here. I did not even reveal its existence to your Marshal Thomas."

Steve nodded. "We'll still need to be careful and to post a guard," he cautioned. "A girl like Felicia would be a big temptation to some of the owlhoots in those mountains."

Alejandro's face darkened in the firelight. "Animals!" he hissed with a fierce vehemence. His big hands tightened on the rifle until his knuckles stood out whitely.

"Not animals—men," Steve corrected. "And all the more dangerous for it."

Alejandro's eyes glittered. "And that is what you hunt—men."

"Right now I'm hunting gold."

Alejandro's teeth gleamed in his grin. "Yes," he said.

"Gold. Have you thought of it, Stephen? Imagined it? Fifty burro loads of gold. How much would that be? How many tons? I've handled financial matters and money all my life. I managed my family's holdings successfully from the time I was a young man. But that is nothing compared to the wealth this gold would represent."

"Felicia and Ramon could become very rich."

"Yes, very rich," Alejandro responded after a moment. "They are very fortunate."

"We haven't found the gold yet."

"No, but I believe it is there and that we will find it. Think what that could mean, Stephen!"

"My wages are enough for me to think about," Steve said.

Alejandro might not have heard him. He stared into the darkness as if he could see there the treasure of which he spoke. Steve looked in the direction of Felicia's tent and was silent.

Chapter Six

Steve saw the riders crest the hill, and something in the grimly purposeful way they bore down upon his party made him rein in Traveler sharply and reach for his Winchester.

"What is it?" Taggar had pulled up beside him, and Steve pointed. The riders were coming at a hard gallop, but they were still too far for him to make out details. Even as he pointed, a flat crack of sound was carried to them on the breeze.

Taggar cursed. There was no doubt now as to the riders' intentions. Foolishly, from that range while mounted, one of the riders had opened fire on them with a saddle gun.

Steve snatched his Winchester free and slid from the saddle in a single movement. "Get going!" he barked at Taggar. "Take them out of here! I'll hold that bunch off!"

Taggar nodded quick consent. His face seemed strained by anger and shock. He reached and caught the reins of Felicia's mare. "Come on!" he shouted, putting spurs to his horse and pulling hers around in his wake.

Steve paid them no more heed. Their attackers were almost in range now. He could plainly count eight of them, although at this distance, identifying them was still impossible. It made no difference. Like hunting, fighting was sometimes necessary.

A shallow draw gave convenient cover, and Steve went to one knee, lifting the Winchester. The afternoon sun was to his left. The attackers were coming out of the north. Their intent revealed, they began to fire now in earnest at their fleeing prey, despite the fact the range was still too great for accurate shooting, particularly from the back of a running horse. The flat cracks of their gunfire carried to him, and he thought he could see gunsmoke being wafted away on the breeze.

He looked around as someone knelt smoothly beside him. Alejandro threw him a predator's grin and lifted his game rifle eagerly.

"Go on with the others!" Steve snapped.

"Nonsense, my friend! I would not miss this even for the gold!"

There was no time to argue. A glance showed him that the other members of the party were rapidly disappearing. The attackers were coming in range. Steve lifted the Winchester again, settling its butt against his shoulder. He knew a moment's passionate yearning for Zeke Spurd's old Sharps rifle with its long-range accuracy, lost now somewhere on the floor of Devil's Canyon. He was conscious of Alejandro taking careful aim down the long barrel of the big-game rifle.

The Winchester kicked against Steve's shoulder as he fired. He felt its recoil travel through his arm. In the distance, one of the charging horsemen threw up his arms and toppled from his horse.

"Ah, first blood to you, my friend!" Alejandro exclaimed with savage envy. Then his rifle went off beside Steve like an artillery piece.

Among the horsemen one figure was punched straight back out of the saddle as if yanked by the loop of a lariat. Alejandro's exultant laughter rang in Steve's ears through the echoes of the shot. "A clean kill!" Alejandro cried.

Two down was apparently enough for the attackers. They scattered, hauling their horses around and racing back in the direction from which they had come. In moments they were out of range. Steve lowered the Winchester.

Alejandro swore in his native tongue. "I was too slow. I should have had another one."

"There's no need," Steve said. "They're on the run." He stood up, and Alejandro followed suit after a moment.

"Who were they?" the Spaniard asked, excitement still evident in his voice and his stance.

"I don't know," Steve said. "They were too far away for me to make out any faces."

The riders had vanished now back over the hill. One of the riderless horses had followed them. The other had fallen to grazing. As he looked, Steve saw a human figure totter uncertainly to his feet.

"Hah! Yours is still alive!" Alejandro exclaimed.

"This isn't some sport!" Steve spat at him savagely.

Alejandro laughed. "You are wrong! It is the hunt, and a good hunter never leaves wounded prey. Come, let's go see our quarry. We might learn something from him."

"We might ride right back into their guns too," Steve said. "Even with two out of action, they still outnumber us. We'll go catch up with Taggar and your wards and put some distance between us and them."

For a moment Alejandro seemed disposed to argue. Then he merely shrugged eloquently. "Very well, Stephen. You are the expert in these matters."

Alejandro looked back out to where the wounded man was trying to reach the sidestepping horse. Steve saw his nostrils flare as if scenting prey. He felt a chill in the summer heat. "Come on," he said.

Steve looked back as they mounted. The wounded man had caught the horse but had not made it astride yet. Steve hoped that his friends would come back for him. Of Alejandro's target there was no sign. Steve remembered the rag doll looseness of the figure being smashed from his horse by the heavy caliber slug. Alejandro, he knew, had been right in his boast. His had been a clean kill.

They overtook the others in good time, and Steve felt something like a hand grip his heart as he saw the look of concern Felicia had for him. He offered only terse explanations for the moment, though. He turned the party once more to the southwest and urged them to a good pace even in the heat. He wanted as much distance as possible between them and their attackers should the latter decide to regroup and come after them. Late in the second day of the journey and they had already run into trouble, he thought grimly. It did not bode well for the remainder of their trek.

He kept them going until past their usual stopping time before finally calling a halt in a cluster of evergreens that had grown over the years around a sinkhole, the soil of which retained the moisture from the heavy spring and fall rains. Leaving the others to make camp, he took Traveler in a mile-wide swing around the grove, scanning the landscape in the fading light. He saw nothing to alarm him, no sign of another human being, only a herd of pronghorn antelope that reminded him grimly of Alejandro's lust for the hunt.

It was almost dark by the time he returned. He was glad

to see that the screen of evergreens concealed the small flame of the cook fire as he approached. Again there was a moment's gratification at Felicia's look of relief at his arrival.

"No sign of them," he answered their questions. "Let's eat and get that fire put out. It's probably not visible through these evergreens, but I don't want to take any chances."

"You think they may be following us, then?" Ramon inquired.

"I told you, I don't want to take any chances. Now, let's eat."

Over coffee after the meal, Steve told them of his fruitless search. Alejandro had already related the account of their skirmish with the attackers. "We'll need to keep a guard posted tonight," Steve finished.

Alejandro nodded his approval, and Taggar asked, "Do you have any idea who they were?"

Steve shrugged and sipped his coffee. It would be his last cup. By his own orders the fire had been extinguished. "Outlaws, robbers looking for victims. There's no telling in this territory." He sipped again, not entirely satisfied with his own answer.

"Why would they attack us?" Felicia asked.

"To kill us and take whatever possessions and supplies we have," Steve answered simply.

"Then you believe it had no connection with the map or the treasure?" Alejandro pressed.

"I don't see how. No one knows about it except us."

Taggar nodded. "That's right." He added, "Unless one of you told someone." The gaze he raked across the others was challenging.

There were quick denials, and then Steve spoke again. "I'd like to see this map," he said to Alejandro.

The Spaniard hesitated a moment, then glanced at his wards. Felicia and Ramon both nodded. "Very well." Alejandro rose to his feet. "I planned to show it to you when we reached the mountains. We will need your help in locating the landmarks."

He crossed to his belongings and fumbled there for a moment, his back to Steve and the others. When he turned, he was holding a heavy bank's money bag complete with lock. He produced a key and undid the lock, resuming his place among them as he spread wide the bag's mouth.

Felicia fetched and lit a lantern as her guardian withdrew a packet from the bag.

Steve leaned forward as Alejandro's deft fingers undid the twine binding the oilskin packet. What he withdrew was a folded parchment. He carefully unfolded it and spread it out before them in the lamplight. It was about two feet square.

At first Steve could make no sense out of the seeming jumble of uneven drawings and patterns. Then Alejandro stabbed one finger down to a series of parallel zigzag lines. "Here," he announced. "These are the mountains."

Steve leaned closer. The map was in good shape for its supposed age, and the images and notations were still clearly legible. With Alejandro's identification of the mountains, Steve began to recognize locales and sites depicted on the map. Devil's Canyon was easily apparent, the length of it drawn in under the mountains with an explanatory notation.

"There is the stone turtle outside the mountains, pointing the way toward the canyon. That will be our starting

point from which the other measurements may be drawn."
An excited tension was evident in Alejandro's voice as he
continued to define various drawings on the map. "And
here and here and here are stone formations and trees
where the symbol of the turtle was also carved."

"How can you be certain about the details?" Steve
asked.

"Captain Vendegas's journal," Ramon said. "The journal and the map give directions and measurements to the
cave from the various landmarks. One must find each
point before proceeding to the next." All of them were
poring intently over the map now.

"And here are the ruins of the settlement where the
miners lived." Alejandro's finger came down on a series
of squares. "They are near the cave here where the smelter
was located. It was sealed by the Indians, but they left a
back passageway untouched, according to the journal."

"What about it, Steve?" Taggar asked eagerly. "Do you
recognize this place?"

"Just a minute." Steve was still studying the map. He
recalled that Taggar had seen the map before.

Ramon explained, "The entrance to the treasure cave
itself is concealed in a cleft in the canyon wall so that it
is invisible without the proper landmarks to measure from
to locate it."

Steve looked up from the map. He saw Felicia watching
him intently. She had not spoken during the discussion
of the map. Her shadowed features, beautiful in the lantern light, were unfathomable.

Steve turned his gaze on Taggar. "I know the general
location of the stone turtle at the base of the mountains,"
he answered the banker's earlier question. Taggar's face
was hawklike in the shifting light. "And I've heard men

tell of seeing the ruins, although I've not done so myself. There's never been a good explanation as to their origin or significance. One old prospector swears that the demons of the devil himself built the original buildings to imprison the lost souls of those who died in the canyon seeking gold. He says he saw the demons late one night. I've always thought he saw the bottom of one too many jugs of moonshine. Others say the ruins are all that's left of a settlement of Mexican miners who supposedly vanished without a trace."

"But they exist?" Taggar was insistent.

"So I've been told. Most of the carved trees are probably gone after this long, but I have seen the carving of a turtle on a stone in the canyon. I never knew what it meant until now."

And did he know even now, Steve wondered. Was this old parchment, with its cryptic drawings, really the key to a fortune in gold, the lost treasure of Devil's Canyon, which had been the subject of countless tales and legends down through the centuries? Here in this camp, clustered with the others around the old map, seeing the expectancy and hope and belief in their faces, it was much easier to believe in the lost cache of Spanish gold than it had been back in Guthrie when he had laughed at the mention of the gold of Devil's Canyon.

"I'd like to see the journal," he said to Alejandro, who seemed to be the designated keeper of the map and, presumably, its companion journal.

Again Alejandro hesitated briefly, drawing a finger along his mustache, before he returned to his pack and bent over it. Steve looked around the camp, realizing that all of them had been preoccupied with the map for some moments now. They would have been easy victims for any enemy approaching the glade of evergreens with even a modicum of stealth. He had been careless in not posting a guard before now. After the attack on them today, such carelessness might easily cost them their lives.

"Ramon," he said, "you take the first watch, starting now. Get your rifle and make a circuit of the glade every few minutes, staying just within the trees and watching the prairie. Don't carry a lantern or light a cigarette. And don't get into a predictable pattern in making your circuits. Vary the time between them and the direction of them. Wake me in two hours and I'll take over."

Automatically almost, Ramon started to protest the tone of the orders. But then he simply nodded in acknowledgement and went to fetch his Winchester. Steve thought the look Felicia gave him contained something of surprised approval in it. He recalled that it had been at her urging that Ramon had approached him the night before.

"Here." Alejandro had returned to the pool of light cast by the lantern. He handed a tattered leather-bound volume to Steve. "The journal of Captain Ricardo Vendegas. It contains his personal diary of his years on this continent as well as notations explaining how the map is to be used."

Steve took the volume carefully. It was in somewhat poorer condition than the map, probably from having been subjected to almost daily use during its owner's sojourn in America. The edges of the binding were worn, and the cover was marked with a dark stain that looked like blood.

He opened the volume at random, the pages crisply delicate beneath his fingers. Immediately his eye fell on an entry dated August 18, 1605. Alejandro had been right, Steve thought. This journal, if authentic, chronicled a Spanish expedition into what was now Oklahoma Territory, and decades prior to what was generally thought the earliest date of Spanish exploration of the area.

The writing was faded, but there was a bold strength to the writer's hand. Steve translated the old, continental Spanish with difficulty:

On the date of this entry the Indians, who had never before disturbed our labors, and against whom we had offered no offense, fell upon us in a bloody massacre. They came upon us like ghosts, and they slaughtered us like veritable demons of Hell. And as such did they appear with their coppery-colored bodies decorated with the most ghastly of paintings of monsters and things of the Pit.

Most of my men, I believe, were at their labors in the mine and had no chance to reach their weapons before they were struck down and mutilated by the pagan savages. May God have pity on their souls. They died fighting as men. And may God have mercy on my soul, for it is on my soul, indeed, as their leader, where the blame rests for this catastrophe. So long had we labored here without disturbance by man or beast that I had allowed us to become lax in our security, leaving us defenseless before the attack. Surely, I must one day suffer the judgment of the Good Lord for my failure.

I myself was in my quarters when the uproar arose. The awful screams of my men still echo in my ears. I ran from my quarters, sword in hand, and was confronted by the frightful visage of a naked savage springing upon me like a beast, knife upraised. I ran him through, but before I could free my sword from his body, a thrown ax struck me and rendered me

*helpless. I lay there, unable to move, and watched my
men slaughtered.*

*I write this now as a prisoner of these godless sav-
ages. Although I have recovered from my wound, I am
just as helpless as when I lay there upon the ground.
I know not if any of my men survived, although I pray
that some did! I know not what fate these pagans have
in store for me, but I am determined that I shall meet
it as a man.*

Steve closed the diary. The translation had been difficult for him, and he felt unclean somehow at reading the
words of a man long dead. Captain Vendegas, he recalled,
had not wanted the treasure ever again to see the light of
day. He had died believing that it belonged to the devil
himself.

Steve passed the book wordlessly back to Alejandro. Let
the Spaniard compare the journal to the map for accuracy,
he thought. He himself was in this only for his wages.

Chapter Seven

"I can see them!" Felicia exclaimed, pointing to the southwest.

Steve did not want to look away from her excited smile. But he pulled his eyes around to follow her finger. In the distance, appearing almost like great banks of clouds on the horizon, were the rugged silhouettes of the Wichita Mountains. "You're right," he told her. "That's the Wichitas."

The two of them rode together at the head of their small column. Steve had detected the mountains some time earlier but had refrained from pointing them out, waiting, instead, for Felicia to spot them herself. He smiled now at her excitement.

"When will we reach them?" She looked at him eagerly, then squinted again at the mountains as if willing them closer.

"Late tomorrow afternoon, I'd guess," Steve told her.

She turned and spoke in hurried Spanish to Alejandro, who rode behind them like a chaperon. Then she studied the distant peaks more intently. "They are small," she said to Steve after a moment, disappointment in her voice.

Steve chuckled. "I suppose they are more like foothills

compared to some of the European ranges or even the Rockies here in this country. But the terrain is rough, and the mountains themselves are a maze of blind canyons, sheer cliffs, and deep draws. You could hide an army in them for a long time with no one the wiser."

"Or a fortune in gold," Alejandro added.

To the north, heat lightning flickered from dark clouds on the afternoon horizon. A breeze rippled the grass, but there was no coolness to it. Rather, it felt like a rush of heated air from some gigantic furnace. There had been no further sign of their mysterious attackers. Although he had maintained a guard since then, Steve had not insisted on their camps being under cover as he had that first night after the attack. He felt certain that the horsemen had been no more than a gang of outlaws who, chancing upon the expedition, had decided to try their luck. If such was indeed the case, then the bandits would have no stomach to try for them again.

They camped that evening in a shallow draw. With the mountains in sight at last, it was tempting to push on to reach them. Felicia suggested as much when he called a halt to set up camp. But distances were deceptive out here, and Steve assured her that a good ride still separated them from the mountains.

Gazing at the distant peaks, Felicia shook her head. "The land here is so open. And yet these mountains just rise up from the prairie where no mountains should be. It does not seem natural."

Steve nodded in agreement. The mountains were, indeed, like rugged islands rising from a sea of grass. Their deep canyons and sheer peaks had long offered the promise of sanctuary to hunted men and the lure of gold to those stricken with a fever for the yellow metal. "We'll reach their base late tomorrow," he said. "And then we'll need to try to locate the stone turtle."

Ramon again took the first turn at guard, as had become his habit. At Steve's direction he stayed within the draw, so as not to skyline himself against the rising moon. A great yellow orb, it heaved slowly up from beyond the horizon, and its luminance cast a pale, ethereal light across the plains.

"Hunter's moon," Steve said. "The Indians would use it to hunt by."

"I thought the American savages were never active during the night," Alejandro remarked. "They are afraid to die during the hours of darkness."

"It depends on the tribe," Steve said. "There's no way you can make very many accurate generalizations about the Indian race as a whole. They are too diverse from tribe to tribe in the way they live."

"You sound as though you admire them," Alejandro said. They were seated around their fire, the evening meal finished. Ramon prowled the outer reaches of the camp.

Steve shrugged. "I don't admire their religious beliefs, but some parts of their way of life have a lot to recommend them."

"You speak wisely, Cazador," a voice said out of the darkness. "Although you should not mock our religions. Even now when they are old, the powers my people worshiped are not so weak as many believe."

Steve had swiveled to his feet, gun leaping into his hand, eyes probing the eerily lit darkness. The others had also risen. The bent, gnarled figure might have materialized out of the moonglow. It came forward now toward the firelight, and Steve forced the tension from his muscles and slid his gun back into its holster. "Velador," he greeted.

The old Indian shuffled into the light. Steve heard Felicia's gasp as the ancient weathered features, the awkward crippled legs, and the gaunt tattooed torso were revealed. In the flickering light of the fire, the hideous, reptilian tattoo seemed to writhe with an unnatural life of its own.

"He's a friend," Steve said, then repeated it as Ramon dashed forward from the darkness, staring in shock at the apparition.

"I am sorry," Ramon gasped. "I did not see him until just now! I do not know how he came past me!"

"Forget it," Steve told him. "He could probably have done the same thing in broad daylight." Once more he marveled silently at the old, crippled brave's stealth.

Reluctantly Ramon withdrew, and Steve gestured toward the fire. "Come, sit with us," he invited the Indian, who had remained standing motionless just within the firelight.

"Huuh." Velador gave his grunt and shuffled forward.

Steve nodded reassuringly to his companions. "This is Velador," he explained. "He is from the mountains."

Velador joined them at the fire. Steve saw that he still carried his bowie and stone ax. But now a flexible bow and quiver of arrows slung across his back had been added to his armaments. His ancient face was inscrutable. Steve felt again the peculiar, probing magnetism of those hooded eyes.

"I am saddened, Cazador," the old brave said at last to Steve. "Saddened that I find you here."

"I have never known you to leave the mountains," Steve said.

"Huuh. There are many things about me that you do

not know, Cazador. Nor does any man of your race. But I know more of you than you might believe."

"I had no intention of bringing sadness to you, Velador." Steve searched the lined features for some indication of Velador's motive for being here.

"I have come to see you." Velador might, indeed, have actually looked into his mind and plucked his thoughts forth. "In the nights, the spirits have told me of your coming. And that coming saddens me."

"Why is that?" Steve asked.

"You come to hunt the gold of Devil's Canyon," Velador said bluntly.

Steve waved the exclamations of his companions to silence. "What gold is that, Velador?" he asked carefully.

"You know. But I will tell you a story of my people and of *el Cañon del Diablo*." Velador's eyes peered out into the moonlit darkness. "Many years ago my people lived in the canyon. It was our home and had been since our earliest times. It protected us from our enemies, for none knew its twists and turns, its caves and secret places, as well as my people. The canyon was our home, and life was good. The old powers were still strong then."

The old man's voice had taken on a mesmeric quality, and Steve pictured the people who had dwelled in the mountains those centuries ago.

"Then, on a certain day," Velador continued, "came the shining ones in their armor, with their long knives and their lust for the yellow metal. At first we did nothing, fearing their strangeness in our foolishness. We watched as they dug great holes in the ground and built buildings in which to live. Some of our people, believing them beings sent by the powers, ventured out to them, only to be seized and put to work against their will in the black holes deep in the earth." Velador's features were briefly, frighteningly, feral in the shifting light.

"Still we did nothing, and the shining ones, knowing now of our existence, began to hunt us for sport, taking our women into their buildings, killing our men or capturing them to work in their mines. It was a bad time for our people."

Steve recalled the claims of Captain Vendegas in his journal that the conquistadores' relations with the Indians had been peaceful. Where between these varying accounts did the actual truth lie? There was no way to know. The truth of the events of those days was lost irrevocably in time.

"And then on a certain day, one of the strong, young braves declared that he would challenge the shining ones and destroy them and release our people and cleanse the canyon from the shining ones' defilement. My people rose to follow that young brave. We fell upon the shining ones and slaughtered them, stopping only when all, save two, had gone down in death before us."

Steve remembered how Captain Vendegas had described their attackers. Almost, he thought, that description might have applied to Velador in his prime. He said nothing as Velador, gazing into the past, continued to speak.

"For a year and more we made those two prisoners work to undo that which they and their brethren had done. Their deep black holes were filled in, their buildings torn down, the cave where they melted rocks to produce gold from the flame was sealed. Then, one day, those last two of the shining ones escaped. Much later one was found dead. But the other disappeared and was not seen again."

"And the yellow metal," Alejandro interjected, his voice thick. "The gold. What of it?"

Velador's head swung toward Alejandro. Although Steve could not see the expression on the old brave's face, the Spaniard paled and was silent. Velador looked away. "The gold we placed in a secret site of my people," he resumed. "So that it might never again see the light of day. It was evil, and the men it brought were evil. We buried it away from the face of the sun to conceal its evil." Velador brooded in silence for a moment.

"But the evil of the yellow metal could not be contained. My people never again regained their strength, and much later others came to seek the gold, weakening my people yet further. Finally, in my own time, the old powers grew weak, and a terrible plague smote my people. Many of them died in agony with great sores on their bodies. That was many years ago. Now only I am left of all my people."

Smallpox, Steve thought. And Velador and only a few others had survived it. Over the years those other survivors had gradually died off, leaving Velador alone in the ancient homeland of his people.

"Still those come who would uncover the gold and its evil," Velador declared. "This one"— he stabbed an accusing finger at Alejandro—"and the child who guards the camp are of the same people as the shining ones. And this other one shares their nature." His finger thrust at Taggar. "And you, Cazador, you have brought them here to search for the gold, and it grieves my heart. Huuh! Do not ask me what gold it is of which I speak!"

Steve stared at Velador for a long moment, then turned his eyes to the flames. They leaped with a golden hue. Was Velador's story true? It confirmed and corroborated much of the account of Captain Vendegas. Did the gold actually exist? And did Velador know its location?

"Can you show us the gold?" Taggar's thought processes had apparently matched Steve's own, and the banker had no qualms about expressing them. "Can you take us to it?"

"The gold is in darkness!" Velador cried with a sudden, fierce vehemence. "No man may look upon it, and its evil shall remain buried."

"I am sorry, Velador," Steve said quietly. "We have come to find the gold. We must search for it. We do not mean to dishonor you or the home and memories of your people."

"Huuh. Remember, I have told you that dark spirits guard the secrets of the canyon. They will protect the gold. I have warned you now. I can do no more. The spirits will do the rest."

"We do not fear the spirits," Steve said calmly.

"Then you are foolish, Cazador. Other men have come searching for the yellow metal, and always the spirits have protected it from them. Their bones lie forgotten in the mountains. It will be no different with you. You are *el Cazador*—the Hunter—and a mighty fighter, but you cannot defeat the dark spirits. They will suck the life from you."

Steve recalled the stories he had mentioned to Felicia—men hunting gold who had disappeared without a trace. He felt his hackles rise.

"I have warned you, Cazador," the old Indian repeated. "Remember my words when the spirits haunt you in the mountains." He rose abruptly with surprising agility, but swayed a little as if the effort had been demanding. "I go," he declared, and he turned to hobble away from the fire.

His departure had come with such abruptness that for a moment Steve was as surprised as the others. Then Taggar gave a muffled oath and got to his feet. He started past Steve's seated position as if in pursuit of the brave.

"Hold it." Steve's words halted him in midstride.

"But he knows where the gold is!" Taggar exclaimed.

Steve shook his head. "I don't think so. He's an old man, and I think he lives in the past as much as the present. Even if he did know, he wouldn't tell us. You heard him. Besides, I doubt that you could find him out there."

Taggar stared out at the prairie. "He's gone," he said. "Just like that." He looked at Steve, then slowly resumed his place at the fire.

"Who was he, Steve?" Felicia was leaning forward intently.

Steve shrugged. "Just an old Indian." The description sounded inadequate even to him. "He's lived up in those mountains for as long as anybody can remember. Mostly he minds his own business, but he's helped me out on occasion."

"His name—Velador, Watcher. Why do you call him that?"

"That's what he's always been called," Steve said. "I don't know where the name came from. I suppose he's called that because he always watches what goes on up in those mountains."

"Do you believe what he said? That it was his people who killed the conquistadores and hid the gold?"

"It could very well be true. He's told me before that Devil's Canyon was the home of his people. And his story corroborates Captain Vendegas's journal."

"What tribe is he from?" Felicia asked.

"Some branch of the Taovayas. They're also called the

Black Pawnees and the Wichitas. That would be my best guess." Steve paused thoughtfully. "But you heard him. His people are all dead. The designations of tribal names for the various groups of Indian peoples are largely the white man's doing. There are whole groups of Indians— clans, family groups, tribes—who have been wiped out by disease or war with the whites, of whom there are no real records. Apparently Velador's people are one of those."

"He didn't like the idea of us looking for the gold," Taggar said.

"He doesn't like the idea of anybody coming to Devil's Canyon for any reason," Steve told him. "The times he has helped me, it has just been to get me out of the canyon that much faster."

"And what do you make of the dark spirits he mentioned, Stephen?" Alejandro's voice seemed somehow remote as he entered the conversation.

Steve shrugged once more. "They're the beliefs of his people. Stories like that always grow up around tales of lost treasures. And the Indians aren't above using their own beliefs to frighten gullible whites away from their lands and totem sites."

"He said the spirits told him we were coming." Felicia's voice had dropped almost to a whisper. "I wonder how he knew we were here?"

"Maybe the spirits did tell him," Steve answered. "But from the tops of those peaks you can see a great distance across the plains, and an open campfire would be visible for miles to someone at that height."

He looked up as Ramon once more approached the fire. The young man's face betrayed his shock as he stared at them. "Where is the Indian?" he asked.

"He's gone," Steve told him.

"But I watched," Ramon said. "I did not see him leave."

Steve didn't reply. He looked in the direction in which the old brave had gone and saw only the pale night. As he had in Devil's Canyon, he wondered if Velador watched them even now.

Chapter Eight

*T*he massive granite wall looming over them made a foreboding black shape against the cloudy night sky. Steve imagined he could feel its weight poised above their camp, awaiting only some otherworldly signal to crash down upon them and obliterate them and their quest. He tried to ignore the feeling, but it persisted, causing him to shift uncomfortably on his blanket.

The raw stone face of the granite hill, first bastion of the Wichita Mountains themselves, was a good quarter mile from their camp. They had spent the last hours of daylight scouring the grassy plain for the stone turtle that, according to the map, pointed the way to the gold. Heat lightning had danced on the horizon, and a furnace breeze had raced across the grasslands.

They had found nothing. The stone turtle, if it actually existed, had eluded their search, although Steve was certain that this was the area where legend and rumor placed it. And without that initial landmark to guide them, following the map would be even more difficult, if not impossible.

The hot night wind wafted a strange scent to Steve's nostrils. He could hear the horses moving restlessly. He stood erect and looked for Ramon, whose stretch of guard duty should be almost over. Then he stiffened. All along the north horizon a curious glow writhed.

"Ramon!" he snapped.

"Here, Steve." The young Spaniard appeared. "I was coming to awaken you. Look there to the north."

"I see it," Steve said. "It's a prairie fire, and we're right in its path. Get everybody up. We've got to strike camp and get out of its way or we'll lose everything."

Including perhaps their lives, he thought grimly as he ran to the picket line where the horses and pack mules were tied. They shifted and shied away from him, nervous at his actions and the unfamiliar glow to the north.

The wind was still strong, which meant that the flames would soon be rushing down upon their camp. Driven by such a wind, fueled by the tall dry grass, such a fire could sweep for miles across the prairie, blinding and suffocating them with its smoke. Steve imagined that he could already feel its heat on the breath of the wind.

Ramon had the others up by now, and the camp was quickly struck, the mules loaded haphazardly, the horses saddled roughly. The fire was clearly visible, rushing across the plain toward them. Its front ran from the base of the mountains for at least a mile to the east, Steve estimated. Now he could feel its heat on the wind. He swung up on a skittish Traveler.

"Which way?" Taggar had pulled his big horse close. He shouted the question above the heated wind and the oncoming roar of the flames. "Into the mountains?"

Steve didn't hesitate. The Wichitas at night offered too many hazards under the best of conditions to be a safe refuge. In that jagged maze of stone they were sure to become separated, and there would be no way they could watch their footing on the precarious rocks. The brush-choked draws and gullies were death traps in which to become caught and suffocated or burned.

"Back to the east!" Steve shouted, waving his arm in that direction. "We'll have to get out from in front of it. Ride!"

Taggar turned and spurred his horse into the night, riding parallel to the line of flame in a desperate bid to outdistance it. Steve saw Alejandro and Ramon go in his wake, the pack mules hard with them. Smoke was already obscuring the cloudy sky, rasping his lungs as he breathed. He coughed harshly.

"Steve!" It was Felicia's voice, fraught with panic. He wheeled Traveler about toward the sound. Frightened by the flames and the flight of the other horses, Felicia's mare shied sideways as she tried in vain to mount. Snorting, tossing her head in fright as she danced away from Felicia, the mare prevented her from getting a foot in the stirrup and swinging up.

Steve pounded his heels into Traveler's sides and sent the stallion leaping forward. He leaned out of the saddle, his reaching hand closing on the mare's reins. Traveler's bulk halted her sideways dance. Instantly Felicia swung up into the saddle. She had managed to put on a blouse and riding skirt. The oncoming flames cast flickering shadows across her lovely features.

"Come on!" Steve drove Traveler forward, still holding the mare's reins. The wiry paint stallion needed no prompting. He stretched into a run. As Steve felt Felicia's mare do likewise, he released his hold on the reins.

Even that brief delay had cost them, he realized. The other members of the party had vanished into the smoke and dark. The flames were close upon them. Squinting

into the heat, Steve knew that there was no way to outflank the line of fire without first angling away from it.

He laid the reins against Traveler's neck, and the stallion swerved in response, heading away from the line of
the fire rather than paralleling it. The pound of hooves and
a glance over his shoulder told him that Felicia rode hard
in his wake. He let her draw even, and then they raced
across the prairie. It seemed to Steve that the fire was actually gaining on them, surging forward to cut them off, the
heat licking at them, the black smoke flushing tears from
their eyes and wrenching hacking coughs from their
throats. He bent low over Traveler and drove the paint
on with heels and voice and will.

Gradually the heat slackened, and the smoke thinned.
Glancing over his shoulder, Steve saw that they were out-
distancing the flames. He slowed Traveler's pace, throwing an encouraging grin at Felicia. She returned it, and
he looked again at the fire. It was almost a mile in width,
and their wild flight had taken them away from it at an
angle. They were in no immediate danger, provided they
did not lose any more ground to its relentless advance.

At last he saw that they had ridden clear of it, outflank-
ing it as an army might outflank an advancing enemy
force. He reined in Traveler, and Felicia pulled her mare
to a halt beside him. They rested for a moment, letting
the horses blow, and watched the fire pass them by.

"Where are the others?" Felicia asked. "Do you
think . . . ?"

"No." Steve did not let her complete the thought.
"Your brother and Don Carlos were with Taggar, and he
knows the range. He cut his teeth on prairie fires. They
had a head start on us and shouldn't have had any trouble
getting clear."

"What started it?"

"I don't know. Maybe the lightning we saw earlier."

"But there was no rain."

"Heat lightning," he explained. "It happens out here sometimes. But there's rarely any rain with it, just clouds and lightning."

"This is a strange land," she said. "Mountains where there should be none, lightning without rain." She shook her head, then looked at Steve again. "How will we find the others?"

"They could be miles from here by now," Steve told her. "Our best bet is to wait until daylight and then return to our campsite. That will be what Taggar does, most likely."

Even in the darkness he saw her drop her eyes and duck her head slightly, as if to avoid his gaze. He realized with sudden contrition that he had just proposed that she spend the night alone with a man not her relative.

"Look," he said, "I didn't mean— Well, we can try to head back to the campsite now."

"No." She shook her head and looked up to his face. "That would be foolish. You are right, of course, and I should apologize. I was being silly. I—" She hesitated, then finished the statement: "I trust you."

Steve smiled, flattered at the simple declaration. "We'll find some cover," he said. "I'll stand watch, and you can get some sleep." He looked away and barely heard her murmured consent. "This way."

They rode without speaking, and a breeze, cool now in the wake of the fire, cleared the last traces of smoke from the air and played refreshingly over them. Steve was extremely aware of the presence of the girl who rode silently beside him, so close that sometimes their legs brushed together. "I trust you," she had said. He swallowed hard and forced himself not to turn and look at her.

A small clump of saplings, clinging to life on the arid plains, offered some sanctuary. He halted Traveler at their edge and dismounted. He loosened the stallion's girth, and Felicia, watching him, copied his actions with her mare. He had his canteens, and he watered both animals from his Stetson, conscious of Felicia standing quietly to one side and watching him.

"You can put your bedroll down over there," he said. "I'll keep an eye on things."

"That's all right. I could not sleep now."

Steve finished with the horses, and, belatedly, remembered to offer her the canteen. She took it with a quiet thanks, but held it for a moment before drinking. "You are gentle with the horses," she said. "Many men are not. Carlos is hard on a horse when he rides it." She broke off as if the thought was unpleasant, and she drank quickly before returning the canteen to Steve. She turned away as he drank, and sat down with her back to one of the saplings. She drew her knees up and wrapped her arms around them.

Steve took another drink. The water was cool in his throat, parched by smoke and dust.

"I am sorry," she said.

"For what?"

"For delaying us back at the camp. I should have been able to mount my horse even though she was scared. I have ridden horses since I was a child."

"Something like that can happen to any rider," he said. Then, to change the subject, he asked, "Did Carlos teach you to ride?"

"No, my father did," she murmured.

Steve remembered that she usually appeared disturbed when the subject of her father came up. He went to her and then sank to his haunches. "What happened to your father?" he asked gently.

"He killed himself," she whispered.

"I'm sorry." Steve wanted to reach out to her. Instead, he lowered himself on down into a sitting position. "I shouldn't have asked."

"It's all right." She shook her head and brushed at her eyes with her fingertips. "I will tell you. I want you to know." She drew a tremulous breath. "I was still just a child. My mother had died when Ramon was small, and my father never remarried. We had land and horses and servants then. I grew up with all those things. That was when Papa taught me to ride. He used to take Ramon and me for long rides across our land. He would pretend to race us and let our ponies beat his Arabian. We both loved him very much." Her trembling lips formed a smile at her memories. Steve remained silent.

"Carlos was Papa's business partner. He had been Papa's friend for as long as I can remember. He owned an estate nearly as nice as ours. We would visit him often, or he would come to see Papa and always bring little gifts for Ramon and me. I knew he and Papa had business dealings, and that he was Papa's friend, and that he was nice to us. As I got older I realized he would propose investments to my father and together they would invest large sums in different ventures such as shipping and timber. They always seemed to be successful. Papa would tell us that we owed much of our wealth to Carlos, because he was so shrewd in choosing investments."

Steve looked away from her toward the horses and then

out over the prairie. The branches of the saplings reached out like ghostly arms and hands.

"Then one day Carlos came to see Papa, very excited about a new venture. It was some kind of shipping venture that sent ships to South America. He had already committed the bulk of his wealth to purchase an interest in the company, but he needed Papa to contribute also, so that between them they would have a—how do you say—?"

"Controlling interest," Steve supplied. He sensed with a grim foreboding where her story was headed.

"Yes, a controlling interest. Papa agreed. Carlos could always convince him. And, in truth, Carlos had rarely been wrong. Papa sold many of our holdings to have the funds Carlos insisted that they needed. So they purchased the company. Carlos was confident that they had done the right thing. But almost immediately there were problems. I do not know everything that went wrong. I could not understand it then, but I knew Papa grew more and more upset. I think he found out that the business was involved in some things that he did not approve of and that Carlos had kept secret from him.

"I do know that there was an awful storm that sank one of the biggest cargo ships owned by the company. It was fully loaded, and there was no insurance. The company already had terrible debts that my father did not know about when he invested. He and Carlos would get mad and shout and yell at each other. It frightened me. I had never heard them fight before. Now it seemed they did it all the time.

"Papa was almost ignoring Ramon and me by then. He acted as if being around us was almost painful to him. I know now that he was ashamed. He did not take us riding anymore because he had sold our horses, even his fine Arabian, to raise the money they needed for the company."

Steve could picture the proud Spanish aristocrat, heir to the fortunes of his forebears, gradually humbled and humiliated, shamed before his peers and his children by the shady financial manipulations of a close friend and trusted business associate.

"The company finally was closed and sold off to pay the creditors," Felicia continued. "I learned later that Papa had spent most of the family holdings in trying to salvage the company. On the day when the last asset of the company was sold, Papa called me and Ramon to him in his study. He told us how sorry he was for failing us and the family. He was crying when he told us. We didn't understand, of course. Then he sent us out of the study. We heard him lock the door, and then after a few minutes there was a shot. The servants had to break down the door." Her voice broke off in a muffled sob.

Now Steve did move, shifting so that he sat beside her, encircling her shoulders with his arm. She leaned against him, almost as if in relief. "And Carlos became your guardian," he finished for her.

She nodded, and then bowed her head. Tears came. Her body was racked by her sobs, and her shoulders heaved beneath Steve's arm. Steve pulled her tighter against him. "It's all right," he told her. "That's all in the past now."

She shook her head almost violently, lifting it enough so that he could hear her next words. "No, it's not all right! I'm scared, Steve."

"There's nothing to be scared about."

"You don't understand." Her voice was muffled. She seemed to make a determined effort to control herself. But still she trembled.

"Why are you scared?" Steve asked, realizing slowly that her story was not finished.

She would not look at him, but he felt her body yield against his. Slowly her tremors subsided. "Carlos has always been good to us," she managed. "He lost much of what he had along with Papa. We had to sell our family's lands, but Carlos was able to invest that money and keep his own family estate, where we went to live with him. He was always good to us," she repeated, as if to emphasize the fact. "He sent me to school and has been teaching Ramon about business."

"Go on," Steve prompted.

Still she would not look at him. "It was when I came home from the school for the first time. I was fifteen and had been away at the school. When I came back Carlos was happy to see me. But I noticed that he looked at me differently than he ever had before. It was hard for me to understand, because I was naive, and I had always thought of him as a kind of uncle, not—not as a man."

Steve felt a coldness that not even the night's heat could dispel. He recalled Alejandro's interruptions when he and Felicia had been together, his veiled warnings to Steve concerning Felicia's virtue. Jealousy, he thought grimly. Not a paternal or even an avuncular concern, but the jealousy of a man who desired a woman. "Did he—" His voice was hoarse.

"He has never done anything," Felicia answered. "But once he said that I should marry him when I became an adult. He tried to make it sound like a joke. But I have seen how he looks at me, and I know he was serious. And I know that if we find the gold, he will not give up. He will want me even more then."

Pain flared in Steve's jaws. He realized he was gritting his teeth so hard that it hurt.

"And now Carlos has lost most of what we had left, as well as his own holdings, in more bad investments," Felicia went on. "That's why we came here. He knew about the map and the story of Captain Vendegas. He is desperate for money now. He had to go deeply in debt for us to come here. I did not want to come, but he demanded that we accompany him. I cannot bear to think of what he will want if we find the gold, and even if we do not—"

At last she lifted her head and turned her face to his. He saw the tears there, and a great, yearning tenderness welled up in him.

"Steve." Her breath was soft on his face. "I'm so scared."

"I'll protect you," Steve said. "Whatever happens, I'll be there, and I'll protect you." Then he lowered his lips to hers. He knew that he meant what he had said.

He held her there until she slept.

Chapter Nine

"What is it?" Felicia tugged on her reins, bringing her mare to a halt.

Steve sat Traveler and stared down at a large flat stone encircled by a ring of smaller stones embedded in the soil. Normally the arrangement would have been all but invisible in the tall grass. But last night's fire had left in its wake only the blackened stubble across which they rode.

"These rocks," he said in answer to Felicia's question. He did not look at her as he spoke. His eyes darted to another flat stone encircled by smaller stones.

"What about them?" Felicia reined closer to him, staring in puzzlement at the rocks.

Steve prodded Traveler to the next stone. "Here's another," he said. Then, as the pattern became clear, he pointed. "And another and another." Excitement surged in him. "Felicia, we've just found our stone turtle."

She gave a little cry of delight.

"See there?" Steve was pointing again. He swung his leg up and over and slid off Traveler. He ran the few steps to one of the other formations. "This is the head, and there are the feet, the shell, and the tail. They're connected by lines of these smaller stones."

Her face lit up as she perceived the pattern. She scrambled from the mare and ran to Steve, hugging him impulsively. He held her for a moment, savoring her nearness, her excitement, the satisfaction of this moment of discovery.

When he released her, she gave him a shy smile. Her face was flushed. The next moment she grabbed his hand and led him as they traced the pattern of stones. The stone turtle was about twenty feet long, he estimated. Eight large flat rocks made up the head, shell, feet, and tail. Each of the large stones was surrounded by smaller stones buried deeply in the soil. Lines of these smaller stones—like cobblestones—connected the feet with the central flat stone serving as the shell.

Steve knelt to examine the shell stone. The pattern itself was obvious. The stones clearly had been deliberately placed here, although how long ago he could not tell. Certainly it had not been any time recently. He looked toward the looming mass of the Wichitas not far distant. Was this ancient stone pattern the key to Captain Vendegas's lost treasure of gold ingots?

The pound of approaching hoofbeats made him stand erect and reach for his Colt. Three riders were coming fast toward them across the blackened plain. Even before their shouted greetings reached his ears, he recognized the other three members of their party.

"Felicia!" Alejandro was first to reach them. He swung down from his big bay even as it skidded to a halt. "Are you all right?" He lifted his hands as if to reach for her shoulders, but she stepped back from him.

"Yes," she answered him quickly. "Steve saved my life."

Alejandro wheeled on Steve. Anger hardened his handsome features. "What is she saying?" he demanded.

Tersely Steve explained. Behind Alejandro, Ramon and Taggar had ridden up. Ramon dismounted and hurried to Felicia. Taggar stayed on his horse, gazing about with a frown.

"You spent the night out here together?" Alejandro snapped in response to Steve's explanation.

"Nothing happened." Steve's voice was cold. "It made more sense to wait for daylight than to wander around in the dark in hope of finding you."

"Forget about it, Carlos." Taggar's voice cut off any further words from Alejandro. "Steve and your ward here have found the stone turtle."

"What?"

Taggar, still astride his horse, gestured. "Look around you." Like Steve, he had detected the pattern of the stones.

Alejandro pivoted toward the mountains like a dog on point, his concerns over the relationship between Steve and Felicia apparently forgotten. "The map and the journal give directions and distances starting from right here," he said breathlessly. "This was the key we needed to make the map work!" Hurriedly he went to his saddlebags and fumbled to extract the map.

Taggar looked down at Steve from his horse. "Good work," he said. "I figured you'd get clear of the fire." He and the other two men, he explained, had not noticed the absence of Steve and the girl until it was too late to turn back. Once clear of the fire, he had prevailed on the other two to wait until morning before moving. Again at his suggestion, they had headed for the campsite, only to spot Steve and Felicia examining the stones.

Steve briefly recounted the story of his and Felicia's escape. He made no mention of what had taken place between them in the small grove of saplings. He had gotten little sleep, dozing intermittently, and waking to check the area for danger. But nothing had intruded on their sanctuary. Awakening in the early dawn, Felicia had smiled at him drowsily. "See?" she had told him. "I knew I could trust you."

Between their two parties, Steve learned from Taggar, they had managed to salvage all their possessions. With the discovery of the turtle, Alejandro insisted they push on into the mountains immediately. Steve did not object. Taggar, still mounted, scanned the plains behind them and raised no protest.

Alejandro took the lead, relying on his interpretation of the map, which he had returned to its packet. They left the charred stubble and rode up a deep draw into the jagged terrain of the mountains.

Straight-line travel was impossible. Steve had to lead them down dry streambeds, around sheer mesas, and along hazardous slopes of slate deeper into the wastes as they sought to follow the ancient map.

"There was a series of trees marked with the sign of the turtle," Alejandro said at one point. "Those were the next landmark on the map." He drew a forearm across his sweating brow.

Steve looked at him grimly. "As I said earlier, I wouldn't count on that being of much help after this long. Even if the particular trees are still in existence, their growth would probably have distorted the carvings to where they'd be impossible to distinguish."

"What do you suggest, then?"

"I've seen a turtle carved on a rock formation. I can take us there if you can identify it on the map."

"Yes! There was such a spot marked on the map. Take us to it!"

They wended their way deeper into the maze. At times they had to dismount and lead their horses over treacherous terrain or double back and seek new paths around the debris of ancient landslides and rockfalls. Steve constantly scanned the surrounding peaks and canyon walls. Gradually he became conscious once again of that eerie sensation of being the target of secretive, peering eyes.

No air stirred in the tangled and broken ground, and the heat bore down upon them with what felt like actual physical weight. Sweat, leeched from their bodies by the oppressive heat, soaked their clothes but seemed to offer no relief. The coats of the horses were streaked darkly with sweat too.

Once, as they skirted the edge of a dense thorn thicket, and their horses pressed close to the canyon wall, Steve saw an enormous rattlesnake. As thick as his thigh and over seven feet long, it slid languidly out of sight in the brush. He eyed the spot carefully, but the huge reptile did not reappear.

At last he led them to the wide mouth of a canyon and reined in near a jutting escarpment of stone. Dismounting, he clambered up the face of the stone to a height of some ten feet. It took him a while to locate it, but his memory had held true. He gazed at the crude shape of a turtle carved into the stone during some bygone year.

In moments Alejandro joined him, clutching the packet with the map as if it were a talisman. Felicia and Ramon peered anxiously up while Taggar continued to scan the canyon rim overhead.

"Yes!" Alejandro was panting slightly either from his exertions or excitement. He traced the weathered carving with a trembling finger. "Three hundred years this has awaited us!" he cried.

"Look out!" Taggar's shout was in the thundering tones he once must have used to make himself heard over the roar of cattle stampedes. "Landslide!"

Alejandro cast a single stunned glance upward. Steve had an image of his horrified face as he wrapped an arm around the Spaniard and carried him from the escarpment in a great plunging leap. A growing roar assaulted his ears even as the pair of them hit ground rolling, the air jarred from their lungs by the impact.

In his wild tumble Steve caught a flashing glimpse of a great mass of stone and earth plunging down toward them from the the cliff face above. In that single fraction of time it seemed to hang suspended above them, blotting out the sky like the disturbing images of his dreams the night before. Then he was somehow on his feet, hauling a winded Alejandro up beside him, conscious of Felicia's scream and of the pounding hooves of bolting horses.

He ran and half dragged Alejandro as the first stones rained around them. One, the size of his fist, struck his shoulder. Another, large enough to crush them both, pounded into the soil close beside them. He heaved Alejandro forward, the force of the effort propelling him along as well. They ran with staggering steps as the ground shook with the terrible impact behind them. Steve kept scrambling, Alejandro moving on his own now. A cloud of choking dust enveloped them.

The thunder faded and they staggered to a halt, chests heaving in the boiling dust. A horse loomed out of the haze. "You made it," Taggar said to them. His chest was heaving also. His horse snorted, its eyes rolling. "And the map is safe too."

Steve saw that Alejandro had held on to the map packet throughout the last few hectic moments. "Felicia? Ramon?" he demanded of Taggar.

"They're fine. We all got clear, even the horses and mules. Not by much, though." Taggar shook his head. "When I saw that slide start, I thought we were all lost."

Alejandro was staring at Steve. "You saved my life," he said.

Steve waved a hand at Taggar. "He saved all of us by spotting that slide in time."

"I had to save the map," Taggar said with a grin.

Hooves clattered on stone, and Felicia and Ramon appeared through the settling dust. Felicia hauled her mare to an abrupt halt and flung herself from the saddle to hug Steve tightly. Returning the embrace, Steve was aware of Alejandro's brooding stare.

Felicia drew back and they released each other. Taggar jogged his horse forward. He returned in a moment.

"The turtle's gone," he reported. "Obliterated."

"It does not matter," Alejandro said. "We know where it was. We can go on from here."

Ramon had dismounted and was standing near Steve and his sister. Now that the dust was clearing, they could see that an enormous mass of earth and rock had torn its way down the face of the cliff, almost blocking the mouth of the canyon.

"What could have caused this?" Ramon said, gazing upward in awe.

"Some animal," Steve suggested. "Maybe a mountain goat. It knocked loose a stone that hit another and in just a few moments caused a major landslide. It doesn't take much in these mountains."

Taggar shook his head. "I don't know. I've never seen anything like it before. It seemed to start all at once."

Felicia sneezed. "Please," she implored. "Let's get out of this dust."

They remounted and circled past the landslide. Taggar was right; the escarpment where the turtle had been carved was buried under tons of rock. If they had been a few moments slower, he and Alejandro would have shared the same fate, Steve reflected grimly.

Alejandro called a halt while he consulted the map and then conferred with Steve. "We are getting closer," he said. The Spaniard's displeasure with Steve seemed once more submerged by his obsession with the gold. His dark eyes held the same glitter as when he and Steve had fought the attacking horsemen. "Perhaps this hunting for gold is better than hunting for beasts," he said. "Do you not feel it, Stephen? The lure of the gold? It is as if I can feel it drawing me on. It is waiting for us there. I know it!"

He neither expected nor needed an answer. Steve had seen it before, had sensed its presence lurking just under the surface in Alejandro. Gold fever, some called it. Indians spoke of the gold love of the white man, the obsession that could claim a man or woman, making the yellow metal more vital to them than family, health, friends, and, even sometimes, life itself. Gold did indeed become the love and lover of such a one.

"We should be close to Devil's Canyon." Alejandro looked to Steve for confirmation.

"Not too far as the crow flies," Steve said. "But we've still got to cover some rugged ground. It might be a good idea to stop here for a while and eat and rest. I make it close on to noon."

Alejandro dismissed the suggestion with an impatient

shake of his head. "There will be time to eat and rest later, after we have found the gold. I told you, the gold is out there not far away. I can feel it in here." He pounded his broad chest, then turned back to his horse.

Steve chewed on a strip of beef jerky as they continued. He was riding somewhat ahead of the others, picking their route. Taggar drew abreast of him. Steve said, "Thanks for the warning back there."

Taggar waved it aside with his customary false modesty. "Forget it. I'm just glad I saw it in time. A terrible thing. One minute nothing, and the next the whole cliff is falling."

"Well, thanks just the same."

"Listen." Taggar spurred his horse closer to Steve's and spoke conspiratorily from the side of his mouth. "Landslides may not be all we have to worry about before this is over."

"Spell that out for me."

Taggar sighed as if in exasperation. He jerked his head toward the others in the column. "I heard some of what Carlos said to you a while ago."

"So?"

"So the man's got it bad. The gold fever. And you know as well as I do that there's no way you can ever trust someone who's got it that bad."

Steve waited him out.

"Look," Taggar went on, the exasperation even more evident in his voice, "I'll help you keep an eye on him. He might be planning some kind of double cross on those kids. Between us we should be able to keep him square."

"Back in Guthrie you thought he was a good loan prospect," Steve pointed out.

"No," Taggar corrected. "I thought this expedition and

the chances of finding the gold were a good loan prospect. I've always had my doubts about Don Carlos, and the more I've seen and heard, the more doubts I have. What's more, I don't like the way he looks at that girl. It's indecent. He's her guardian, for heaven's sake!" He paused a moment, but Steve still gave him no response. "Well, what do you say?" Taggar urged. "You and I together can keep on him, right?"

"I'll think about it," Steve said, then added, "And in the meantime, keep it quiet or you might find yourself at the wrong end of the don's big-game rifle. He's not the kind of man who'd take kindly to some of what you just said."

"I can handle myself. I've done it for years," Taggar said.

Steve didn't argue. "Let's just try to find the gold." He kicked Traveler on ahead.

Finally Steve did call a halt, to rest the horses in the shade of a great stone pinnacle. Alejandro fretted, but occupied himself with the study of the map and the journal. Steve ran his eyes along the rocky hills that they had just crossed.

"Do you see anything, Steve?"

He turned to regard Ramon, who had approached him. The young Spaniard seemed more self-confident than when Steve had first met him. Gone was the facade of juvenile bravado. It had been replaced by something of greater depth and substance.

"No," Steve said. "I don't see anything. But out here you can never afford to let your guard down."

"Like in a fight, *sí?*"

"Yeah, like in a fight."

"Have you ever been beaten in a fight, Steve? Like I was in Guthrie?"

Steve grinned. "Not lately. But I've ended up on the floor or in the dirt more than once."

Ramon nodded thoughtfully and appeared to ponder his next words carefully. "Have you ever had to fight someone again after he has beaten you?" he asked finally.

"Once or twice," Steve admitted.

"And what happened?"

"One time I won. The other time I just got whipped again."

Ramon nodded seriously. "And were you scared?"

Steve realized that Ramon's questions, as on that first night in camp, required more than simple answers. He said, "A man's a fool not to be scared if he's going up against someone who's bigger or stronger or faster than he is, or who has beaten him before. Basically I've got two rules about fighting, Ramon. First, always try not to fight unless you're on your own ground and you know you can win. But sometimes you're going to have to fight, anyway. And that's where the second rule comes in. When you have to fight, then it's just like anything else in life. You put your faith in God and do your best, regardless of whether or not you're scared. If a man does that, he's got nothing to be ashamed of whether he wins or loses."

"I think I understand," Ramon said. "I have been thinking that if I should ever have to stand up to Bruiser Jackson again, that I would be afraid of him. But I see now that that does not really matter so long as I fight him when I have to."

"Remember what I said about keeping it on your own ground if you can," Steve said. "Don't try to match fists with a man like Jackson. If he's out to kill you, use your knife. Then you're on your own ground. You had the right idea when you fought him before. You just waited too long to act on it."

"Thank you, Steve." Ramon turned away.

"Let's go, *mis compadres,*" Alejandro called. "The gold is awaiting us!"

The gold and what else? Steve wondered as they moved out of the pinnacle's shade and into the brutal heat trapped by the granite walls. He thought of the prairie fire the night before, and of the landslide only that morning. So far they had encountered no human enemies in these mountains, but that really did not matter. The hand of nature itself seemed set against them in their quest.

Chapter Ten

El Cañon del Diablo. Devil's Canyon. Source of legends of lost gold and vanished men. Reputed abode of the dark and vengeful spirits of a vanished people. And the secret resting place of an ancient cache of Spanish gold? Steve wondered about that as he led his fellow seekers into Devil's Canyon.

A brooding silence as heavy as the heat seemed to lie over the canyon. The sense of being observed tingled more strongly than ever at Steve's nerves. No birds flew, no reptiles or other animals scurried for cover in the brush. The canyon appeared strangely deserted, as if it were awaiting their arrival. Steve had the sudden gripping sensation that he was riding into a trap.

His eyes scanned the canyon walls, probing into the brush. When he had ridden here after Zeke Spurd, he had known what kind of trap awaited him and who his enemy was. But who or what was the enemy now? Velador's dark spirits? Or some other human enemy, all too tangible but as yet unknown?

His instincts, honed by hard-won experience, had been right that other time, and, as he had on that other occasion, he loosened the Winchester in its sheath.

110

He led them deeper into the canyon. He estimated that they were past the halfway point when the canyon floor widened out before them. Low brush and scrub oak choked the flat, open area. The still waters of a pond lay in the shadow of the canyon wall.

"The ruins should be here," Alejandro announced, anger and frustration straining his voice. There was no sign of human habitation anywhere on the canyon floor.

"There could be anything concealed in that brush," Steve pointed out. "And the Indians supposedly had the settlement buildings torn down. Form a line across here and we'll see what we can find."

Spread out across the width of the canyon, they urged their horses through the low brush and around the scraggly trees. It was Taggar, near the pond at the base of the canyon wall, who called out.

They gathered around him where he sat his horse, and gazed down at a barely discernible pattern of stones half buried in the ground. Steve realized that he was seeing all that remained of the ancient foundation of some forgotten structure. As he looked, he could detect other foundations and, partially obscured in a dense thicket, a section of crumbling wall.

"Yes." Alejandro's voice was husky. "Yes."

They dismounted and spread out through what was left of the ancient settlement. Most of the structures were some ten by twenty feet in size. They had been constructed of sun-dried bricks, now eroded by the elements to piles of fragments scattered about the foundation stones.

Steve counted a dozen structures. He tried to picture this wide area of the canyon floor cleared of brush, with the low adobe buildings close to the pond to house the Spanish miners and, if Velador was to be believed, their captured Indian women. He shook his head, unable even to visualize what it must have been like in that centuries-gone community.

Yet it had existed. The stone foundations and crumbling bricks gave testimony to the achievements of those hearty and ruthless adventurers who had sought out new lands for glory and conquest.

To his right, Felicia gave a little exclamation, and she knelt to brush leaves and dirt away from something. Steve went to her and saw the dull gleam of weathered metal showing through the soil. Kneeling beside her, he withdrew his bowie and excavated the object.

It was a solid chunk of iron in a rough cone shape with a flattened top surmounted by a thick arch. Steve hefted it in both hands, guessing its weight to be at least twenty-five pounds.

Alejandro approached as he saw them examining it. He gave a grunt of recognition.

"What is it?" Felicia asked.

"A tether weight," Alejandro answered, gazing hungrily at the object as if it were made of solid gold. "The conquistadores used them to tether their horses. The reins were tied to the arch there. Let me see it for a moment." He took it from Steve's hands, turning it one way and another, peering at it closely. "Ah!" he exclaimed in triumph. "There is an engraving on it. See?" His finger traced barely discernible lines.

"The head of a knight!" Felicia said in excited recognition. "With a plume in his helmet."

Steve could make out the worn figure engraved on the iron. Here, he thought, was the answer to the riddle of who had built the ancient village. Three centuries ago Spanish conquistadores had, indeed, lived in this canyon.

"Over here," Ramon called from the edge of the wooded area.

They found him standing over a shallow depression some ten feet wide. Little vegetation had grown there because of the jumble of chunks of stone of varying sizes that paved it.

"The mouth of a mine!" Alejandro cried. "Filled in with rubble, exactly as the journal says!"

Over the years the debris used to fill the shaft would have settled, Steve thought, resulting in exactly the phenomenon they observed.

Alejandro had brought the heavy iron tether with him, carrying it by the arch with one hand as if reluctant to release this proof of the conquistadores' presence. Now he dropped it carelessly and looked longingly up at the cliff face. "The smelter cave was up there," he said. "They buried it in a landslide."

Steve could detect no sign of a cave. But even the centuries had not erased a wide scar down the granite wall where once tons of stone must have been broken loose to plunge to the canyon floor. Penetrating that giant pile of rubble would be impossible.

"There's supposed to be another entrance they left unsealed, isn't there?" Taggar's voice was slightly hoarse.

"Yes! This way!" Alejandro hurried along the canyon wall, stumbling in his haste on the uncertain footing. Taggar followed eagerly.

"I will bring the horses, Steve," Ramon offered. Steve nodded approval. He did not like the idea of being too far from his saddle gun and their supplies.

Alejandro and Taggar were peering at a natural hollow in the wall of the canyon. It was studded with boulders and slanted upward almost to the rim. A short boulder-strewn ledge extended along the cliff face from the top corner of the hollow.

"The entrance is up there on the ledge." Alejandro pointed to the spot.

They clambered up the slope of the cut until it ended in a sheer stone face. The dark shadow of a crevice leading to the ledge some fifteen feet above was visible in the wall of the cut.

"I'll go up," Steve said. Alejandro nodded, and Steve made his way to the crevice. It would be cramped, he saw, but the sides offered plenty of hand and footholds.

He squeezed into the narrow space, feeling a constriction in his chest, as if the stone walls had begun to close together with him between them. He shook the feeling from himself, reaching up to find a grip for his hand. Slowly, hold by hold, booted feet kicking for purchase or bearing down hard on small promontories, he hauled and levered himself up the crevice. He heaved himself finally onto the ledge and squatted a moment, resting.

From this vantage point high up on the canyon wall, he had a good view of the brush and the pond. He even imagined that he could make out the square foundations of the old town. On the opposite wall of the canyon, clumps of vegetation clung precariously to the naked stone. Looking back down into the hollow, he saw that Ramon had brought the horses into the mouth of the cut and tethered them there among the boulders.

"Well, Stephen?" Alejandro's voice, echoing from the walls of the hollow, carried a ring of impatience.

Steve got to his feet and carefully examined the ledge, making his way around the boulders. Even looking for it, he almost missed the black shadow at the base of a boulder. It became the mouth of a hole half obscured by the thorny limbs of a bush. With his bowie he chopped the bush away, revealing a hole some three feet in diameter. It angled down into darkness.

He returned to the end of the ledge. "It's here, I think," he reported. "I'll need a lantern."

Ramon brought the lantern to him, scrambling agilely up the crevice walls. He watched in silence as Steve lit the lantern and extended it into the hole. The flame dimly illuminated a rough walled passage going downward at a steep angle.

The dark hole seemed to beckon Steve. "I'm going down," he said.

Quickly he secured the rope to one of the boulders and tossed the rest of it down into darkness. The angle of decline did not really look steep enough for him to need the rope, but he didn't want to run any risks that he could avoid in this undertaking. He drew the bowie and dropped to his knees, peering once again into the dark tunnel. Still he could detect nothing.

Bowie in fist, pushing the lighted lantern awkwardly before him, he crawled down into the blackness. *"Vaya con Dios,"* came Ramon's voice from behind him.

Go with God, Steve translated. Go with God into the Canyon of the Devil.

Some ancient flaw or fault in the stone, he realized quickly, had at some point been smoothed and shaped by human hands to create the tunnel through which he crawled. Who had done it and why? The Spaniards? The Indians? And why had this entrance to the smelter cave been left unsealed by the Indians after the massacre of the Spanish miners? Perhaps because it did not really lead into the smelter cave, he thought. Perhaps even now he crawled only deeper and deeper down a tunnel that led into the bowels of the earth, maybe into hell itself. What better site for an entrance to hell than the Canyon of the Devil?

The lantern's writhing flame revealed the damp stone walls, chipped and scarred in places during some past age by human tools. He brushed through a spider's web spanning the passage, and he saw the creature scuttle away from the light. He thought of giant rattlesnakes that would be drawn to such a place as this for a den. The hilt of the bowie was wet with his sweat. He thought of landslides and earthquakes that could seal or collapse the tunnel, leaving him entombed. And he thought of dark spirits dancing in the blackness. *Vaya con Dios.* . . .

Tiny red eyes glared at him from the darkness ahead. He thrust the lantern forward and saw furry hindquarters and a naked scaly tail scampering away. Well, rats were better than dark spirits, he supposed.

The slope of the tunnel became more steep. He had to hold the lantern's base to keep it from tumbling on ahead, and to brace himself with aching muscles to keep from doing the same. His knees felt raw from contact with the stone floor, and he was sweating heavily despite the cooler temperature here below ground. He could no longer see the mouth of the tunnel behind him, although he could not recall the tunnel having curved away from it. He let his hand brush occasionally against the rope he had tossed ahead of him. How long had he been down here? How far had he come?

Abruptly the tunnel leveled out. Before he had gone two yards farther, the tunnel walls disappeared from the lantern's illumination. He sensed open space around him and realized he had come out of the tunnel into a larger chamber. Using the bowie, he probed the space above his head.

Finding no ceiling, he rose cautiously to his feet, lifting the lantern high.

Gradually he was able to make out a large chamber some fifty feet square. Its walls and floors, like the tunnel, also showed signs of improvement by human hands.

A dark jumble of shapes against one wall drew his attention. He moved carefully forward. His nostrils flared at the acrid stench of what he recognized as guano—bat droppings. He guessed he was walking on a layer of the stuff. An eerie rustling of movement overhead confirmed his guess that this cave, whatever its past function at the hands of man, served now as a sanctuary for the winged mammals.

The jumble of shapes proved to be a corroded pile of twisted metal, most of it unrecognizable. He saw several large crucibles, like great metal bowls, and he realized that he was looking at the remains of the ancient smelter. The crucibles had been used to melt down the gold ore taken from the mine so that it could be cast into ingots.

Beyond the remains of the smelter was what seemed to be a deep pit almost filled with a fine powdery substance. Kneeling, he examined its consistency with his fingers. This was the pit where the ashes from the smelter fires had been dumped. How deep did the pit go? With the tunnel to serve as a chimney, and with the mouth of the cave unsealed to allow circulation, the cavern would have made an ideal site for the smelter.

Rising, he made a slow circuit of the room. He paused near what he guessed had been the cave mouth, marked now by a pile of rubble. No slight gleam of daylight filtered through the mass of earth and stone. The Indians' job of sealing the cave had been thorough.

Something pale and whitish gleamed in the lantern light

to one side of the piled stones. Steve stepped closer and lowered the lantern. He recoiled slightly as the flame revealed a human skull leering up at him. There were more bones, a jumbled mass of them.

One skeleton alone was almost complete. The lantern light shone dully from the dented breastplate still in place across the rib cage, the tarnished helmet lying beside the skull. The shining ones, Velador had called them. Here lay the remains of one of the Spanish conquistadores.

Among the jumble of other bones Steve detected fragments of leather clothing and stone weapons like those of Velador. Indians and their final victim, Steve realized. The Spaniard had not died easily; parts of at least three other skeletons surrounded his own.

Looking more closely at the skull above the breastplate, Steve saw that it had been fractured, perhaps by the same blow that had torn the helmet loose. Beside the armored figure's hand lay the hilt of a sword, its blade still encased in the rib cage of one of the Spaniard's enemies.

Steve reached for the hilt of the weapon, then stayed his hand. Some things were best left undisturbed. Carefully he backed away from the gleaming bones, testimony to ancient violence. Perhaps the deaths of the braves here in the cave explained, in some way, the Indians' decision to leave the tunnel unsealed.

The black mouth of another passageway revealed itself in an adjoining wall. He ventured down it a few steps, seeing that it diminished quickly to a low-ceilinged chamber with no other access. More equipment from the smelter operation had been stored here. Its jumbled shapes cast distorted shadows on the walls.

Something else seemed to move on the wall. Steve peered closer. Faintly, the colors still dimly visible, he discerned simple drawings on the wall. Stylized stick figures chased and slew curious horned beasts. Plainly the cave had been in use long before the Spaniards had appropriated it for their own purposes.

Had the primitive paintings been done by Velador's people? Or were they the work of some even more ancient race that had roamed the canyon when these mountains were yet young?

Steve withdrew from the passage. He thought he saw one of the stick figures leap to thrust its lance at its prey in the last flickering light of the lantern.

He had spent enough time here, he decided suddenly. The gold, if gold there was—and the smelter certainly argued for it—had been long removed from this place of dead men and forgotten dreams.

For a moment the small mouth of the tunnel eluded him, and the cold feather of incipient panic brushed down his spine. Then he saw the rope, the last coils of it just within the chamber, and he went thankfully to the tunnel.

The return was a scrambling, scratching climb up the narrow passageway, juggling the lantern, the bowie back in its sheath now. At times he had to resort to the rope to haul himself upward, the stone floor wet and slick beneath his feet. At last he saw the glare of daylight ahead and knew a draining relief. He had not realized how deeply into the earth he had gone.

With the circle of daylight as his goal, he scrambled and pulled himself hurriedly on, emerging at last into the blinding glare of the sun. Ramon extended a strong hand to assist him the last few feet.

He was just straightening to his full height when the gunshot came, simultaneous with the bullet chipping rock by his head.

Chapter Eleven

Steve lay flat on the ledge, staring out at the far wall of the canyon from which he thought the shot had come. Ramon had flung himself down almost as quickly as Steve. The Spaniard twisted about to lay hold of one of the saddle Winchesters from their horses.

"I asked Carlos to pass this up to me while you were in the tunnel," he explained with a quick grin.

"*Muy bueno,*" Steve said, reaching for the rifle. He could only hope Alejandro and the others had taken cover among the boulders in the hollow, for now he must concentrate on their would-be ambusher.

He was not certain where the enemy was located, but he thought he had detected powder smoke drifting up from a clump of brush on a ledge on the far wall of the canyon. Focusing on that spot, he nodded to himself after a moment as sunlight gleamed off metal and a vague shape moved behind the concealing bush.

Still flat on his stomach, Steve jammed the butt of the Winchester against his shoulder, sighted with a brief glance, then saturated the brush with bullets. On the far wall of the canyon there was a thrashing in the thicket.

Then a man lurched forward and plummeted earthward, rifle tumbling beside him as he fell.

Ramon exhaled sharply at Steve's side and started to push himself erect. Steve shoved him flat again. "Stay down," he ordered. As Ramon looked at him with startled eyes, Steve added, "Go call down to the others and tell them to stay under cover and be ready. I don't think this is over yet."

Ramon nodded and writhed away along the ledge. The boulders here gave ample cover, Steve thought, which was all that had protected him from that first shot.

Steve scanned the far wall of the canyon and the brush-choked floor with careful, penetrating eyes. He saw nothing. He heard Ramon calling down to the others and heard Taggar's voice answer.

Ramon came squirming back. "They are all right," he reported. "They have done as you said."

Steve nodded, still searching the canyon for signs of life. "Watch the far wall and the canyon floor," he said. "Take your time and look for movement or any shape that doesn't seem natural."

"You think there are more of them?"

"I'm certain of it."

"What do we do?"

"What I said," Steve answered. "Watch and wait."

Nothing moved in the canyon. The gunshot echoes had rumbled away into silence.

"Lawton!" The voice bounced back and forth between the canyon walls, its source impossible to locate.

Steve drew a deep breath. He could not tell where the voice came from, but he knew whose voice it was. He waited for the reverberations of sound to die. "Starr!" he shouted back in acknowledgement.

"I want a parley, Lawton," the voice returned. This time there was no mistaking it. The unseen speaker was Joe Starr.

"We've got nothing to parley about, Starr," Steve shouted back. "Ride out, or we'll kill you to a man!"

"Just you and me," Starr responded. "No guns. Just a few minutes of talk."

"Forget it, Starr!"

"Better think about it, Lawton. You're outnumbered."

Steve searched the canyon's floor and walls for some sign of the gunman. But he could spot nothing. Starr was far too wily to reveal himself at this point. "We can talk from here!" he called. He, likewise, had no wish to reveal himself to the guns of Starr and his men.

"Face-to-face, Lawton! That's how it's got to be."

Steve considered. As it stood now they were stalemated, with the odds in numbers undoubtedly in Starr's favor. Further, Starr had them located, while they had no idea of the whereabouts of Starr and his men.

He glanced at the sky. Late afternoon. It had been a long day, he thought wearily. But with night the advantage might well shift to them against Starr's men. A parley would buy time and just might give them more information about what odds they faced. He was aware that Ramon was watching him tensely.

"All right, Starr!" he shouted. "Just you and me. But I keep my gun. You show yourself unarmed."

Sardonic laughter rang down the canyon. "You're crazy, Lawton."

"Take it or leave it," Steve returned. "It's the best you'll get."

"How do I know I can trust you?"

Steve gave a short bark of laughter. "I'm the one who

should be asking that. But you have my word. No one here starts anything."

"Your word's good enough for me," Starr called finally. "How do we work it?"

"Give me five minutes. Then show yourself, hands up and no guns. Got it?"

"You're a hard man, Lawton!"

"Got it?" Steve shouted again.

"Yeah, I got it."

Steve looked at Ramon. "Carlos said you can use one of these." He pushed the Winchester toward him. "Is that right?"

Ramon nodded. "*Sí.*"

"Okay. When I get out there, cover me. Use your own judgment, but try not to fire the first shot."

"I understand." Ramon hesitated. "Is it safe for you to go out there?"

"No, but it's not safe to stay here, either. Maybe I can learn something. Remember, let them make the first move."

"Yes."

Leaving him there, Steve crawled to the crevice and slid down it. Alejandro met him at its base. The don's eyes were alight. He carried his big-game rifle with an avid readiness. "I heard, Stephen," he said eagerly. "It is a good plan! Once he is in sight—" He grinned savagely and hefted the big rifle.

"No!" Steve said sharply. "No one starts anything on this side. I want to hear what he has to say." He looked past Alejandro to Taggar, who had joined them, Winchester in hand. "Understand me?"

Taggar's nod came without hesitation. Alejandro's was

slower, made with reluctance. "Very well, Stephen. It shall be as you say."

"Just don't forget it." Steve went past them, moving carefully down the steep slope of the hollow.

Felicia came forward, her face concerned. She did not try to stop him. "Be careful," she said softly.

He crouched behind a boulder at the mouth of the cut and studied the terrain. The five minutes were almost up. Motion in the underbrush caught his eye. The next moment Joe Starr stepped into view. He walked forward until he was well clear of the brush, then raised his hands briefly to shoulder height before dropping them back to his sides. The holster on his wide, tooled gun belt was empty.

Steve waited a moment, then straightened, stepped out from behind the boulder, and started forward. Starr watched him come. Steve reflected that he felt more secure with Ramon, inexperienced as he was, above him on the ledge than he would have with either Alejandro or Taggar in that position.

Starr was in trail garb. His lip curled in his habitual sneer as Steve approached. He spread his hands, palms up. "See? Just like I said. No guns. Just you and me."

"Get on with it." Steve had halted some six feet from the gunman. He resisted the temptation to look about. The real danger was right here in front of him.

"Now, is that any way to greet a business associate?" Starr's tone was mocking.

"What kind of business?"

Starr's mouth thinned, the sneer falling away. "All right," he said. "I'll make it simple. All we want is the map. Give it to us and you ride out of here free and clear."

Steve held his face immobile. "What map?"

The sneer returned. "Don't play me for a greenhorn,

Lawton. Either you hand over the map or me and the boys will come take it away from you."

"You wouldn't stand a chance. We've got the cover. We'd cut you in half before you could root us out."

Starr shrugged casually. His dissolute face with its fledgling jowls was cruel. "Maybe. Maybe not. But either way you're putting that pretty little Spanish gal to a heck of a risk." He leered. "Particularly if you lose and she's still alive."

Steve didn't go for the bait. "I'll give you one chance," he told Starr. "Ride out of here now with your boys and we'll let you go." He was acutely aware that he was probably the target of at least one unseen rifleman at that moment.

Starr chuckled. "You got it wrong, *amigo*. It's me giving you the chance to hand over the map—and then I'll let *you* ride out. I'll even let you take the little Spanish filly out with you. But if you don't give me the map, we'll take it from you."

"You think you can do better than you did the first time?"

Starr's black eyebrows lifted sardonically. "So you figured out it was us who came down on you outside of Guthrie?"

Steve shrugged. "When you showed up here, it was obvious. That was a fool move the other day—firing on us from that range from horseback."

"New man," Starr explained. "He started shooting way too early. I probably would've killed him myself if one of you hadn't. He looked like an artillery shell hit him."

"Big-game rifle," Steve told him. "The don favors it."

Starr grunted. "Well, when that didn't work we just rode hard day and night and got here ahead of you. Then we sat and waited. When you stopped here we got into position."

"You haven't done too much better this time around," Steve pointed out. "That sniper you sent up there to pick me off was a little overeager too."

"I told him to be sure to get you first. I guess he just couldn't wait," Starr said. "And it took him too long to get into position. Too bad I couldn't have used old Zeke Spurd."

"He didn't do very well, either."

"That's right, isn't it?" Starr appeared genuinely amused. "But we've still got the numbers on you."

"Maybe for a while," Steve conceded. "But after nightfall I'll be coming out here after you. With this." He tapped the hilt of the bowie.

"I believe you'd do it too. I've heard the stories about you, Lawton. Are you really as good as they say?"

"Better."

Starr chuckled, but his eyes were hard. "Well, Simon and Luther would still like to try you out, but straight up with handguns. Not out here in the brush at night."

"They may not have the choice." Steve's voice was low. "Ride out of here with your boys. You can't get to us, and we won't hand over the map."

"You're a tough man to deal with, Lawton." Starr let his shoulders slump in apparent defeat. He fumbled behind his wide gun belt. "Smoke?"

Steve's gun came up in a single smooth movement, its hammer clicking back. "Pull it out and drop it, Starr. Carefully."

Starr stared at Steve. An ugly, vindictive rage flared in his eyes as he cursed Steve.

"You heard me," Steve said coldly. "Take it out and drop it."

Slowly, his face a mask of anger, Starr pulled the small two-shot derringer from its place of concealment behind his wide gun belt. He dropped it to the ground. At Steve's command he kicked it away.

Steve kept his gun leveled. "Now let's get back to your choices," he said. "The only reason you wanted to talk to me at all was because you knew you couldn't pry us out of that hollow. And nothing's changed. I could have killed you for your stunt just now. I probably should have. But it's easier if I let you live and you take your boys out of here. That's your only choice."

Starr nodded with bitter resignation.

"We'll want to see you and your men ride past here on the way out," Steve told him. "And I'll have a good man with a rifle up there keeping watch to make sure you don't come back. Don't try to leave anyone behind. You'll only get him killed."

Starr stared at Steve for a long moment, his eyes hateful. Steve expected some last threat or curse. Instead, Starr glanced briefly at the mouth of the hollow, and then he turned and walked toward the underbrush. Steve rushed away, his pistol leveled at Starr's retreating back. He felt suddenly extremely naked and vulnerable here in the open.

Then he was back in the cover of the cut, Felicia darting to him. Quite naturally his arm encircled her shoulders, pulling her briefly against him. He ignored Alejandro's challenging stare as he resheathed his Colt.

"Stay under cover," Steve ordered. "They'll be riding out of here soon. Keep them under your guns, but let them go."

"That was Joe Starr from Guthrie, wasn't it?" Taggar asked.

"Yeah. They've been on our trail since we left."

"And you think he'll give up this easy?"

"For now, anyway. I'll follow them a ways down the canyon just to be sure they're really pulling out. Starr doesn't have any stomach for a real fight, and he knows we could give him one as long as we hold this hollow. We'll stay here tonight. After that we'll just have to take our chances."

"You should have let me kill him!" Alejandro cried. "I had him in my sights!"

"Looking for another trophy?" Steve asked. "If Starr had been shot, then one of his boys would've taken me down too."

Alejandro turned away sharply. Steve had caught the dangerous glitter in his eyes, and he wondered if the turn of events he had described might not have suited the Spaniard's unspoken desires. And, he wondered with a sudden chill, had Starr been the only target Alejandro had kept in his sights?

"They are coming!" Felicia had moved to the mouth of the hollow to keep watch.

"All right. Get back. Everybody take cover." Steve knelt on one knee behind a tall rock. His .45 was once more in his hand.

He heard the clatter of horses' hooves ridden at a lope just short of a gallop. Any faster pace over the rough terrain would have been foolish. Starr came first, riding a big sorrel. His body was rigid with suppressed anger. He looked neither to the right nor the left. Close at his heels, mounted on all but identical bays, were the twin figures of Simon and Luther Meade. The two gunfighters still wore their pale buckskins. Like their chief, they rode past without a sideward glance.

The huge figure that came next was unmistakable. Unlike his fellows, Bruiser Jackson cast an angry gaze into the hollow as he swept past. The final rider was a stranger to Steve. He had an impression of a tanned face and a low-slung .45 on the man's thigh.

Then they were past, their clatter diminishing rapidly down the canyon. Five in all, Steve mused. So Starr had not really outnumbered them, as he had stated.

Taggar came to the mouth of the cut. "I'll follow them," he said. "That way you can stay here and keep an eye on things."

Steve shook his head. "No. It's my job; I'll do it." He met the banker's gaze. After an interval Taggar shrugged and turned away.

Steve gave quick instructions to Ramon, then changed his riding boots for the flexible Apache moccasins. On foot, Winchester in hand, he set out at a job in the wake of the riders. The trail was easy to follow. He did not want to get too close, only to assure himself that Starr and all his men were really gone.

Starr seemed to be keeping his word. Not far from the canyon's mouth, Steve turned back. For now, he was certain that Joe Starr would leave them alone.

Chapter Twelve

"**R**amon's still up on the ledge," Taggar said. "I'll take his turn at guard duty down here." The banker had risen from the fire, which he shared with Alejandro and Felicia far back in the hollow. With his Winchester carried casually at his side, he started toward the mouth of the draw past Steve, who lounged easily against a tall boulder.

Steve waited until Taggar was even with him. "Hold it, Taggar," he said.

Taggar paused, turning toward Steve. His expression was questioning. "Yeah?" he said.

Steve straightened away from the rock. He had been waiting patiently since night had fallen. Now his wait was over. "Let's forget posting a guard for now. Your boys won't be back."

"Won't be—" Taggar broke off as he understood the full significance of the Steve's words. "What do you mean—'my boys'?" His face showed only puzzled interest, but disguising emotions was something any good banker or politician could do with ease.

"I have just a few questions," Steve said. "Set your rifle down, why don't you?"

Taggar hesitated, then leaned the Winchester carefully

against a rock. He kept his eyes on Steve's face, obviously trying to read what was behind Steve's words, and, just as obviously, failing. Bankers and politicians weren't the only ones who could conceal their emotions, Steve mused grimly. Sometimes a Texas Ranger's life depended on that same skill.

"All right, Steve," Taggar said easily. "What's on your mind?"

Steve was aware that Alejandro and Felicia, sensing the tension between him and Taggar, had moved to within earshot of their voices.

"A few questions," Steve repeated.

Taggar showed his uplifted palms in a disarming gesture. "Ask them. If I have the answers, you're welcome to them."

"Am I?" Steve said. "Well, try this. When I was out there talking to Starr, he said that all he wanted from us was the map."

"So?" Taggar still looked bewildered.

"So," Steve said carefully, "how did Starr even know there was a map?"

Taggar shrugged. "Who knows? Maybe he heard rumors back in town. There's always talk that goes around."

Steve shook his head. "Not good enough. You made a point of telling us to keep quiet about the map. You said yourself that no one in town even knew about it except the five of us."

"And you think I let it slip?"

"No, I don't think you let it slip," Steve said. "I think you told Starr deliberately when you hired him to follow us and kill us so you could have the map for yourself."

"That's crazy!"

"Is it?"

"Any of us could have let that slip in town where Starr picked it up. It could have been Carlos, the girl, or that fool kid."

"I don't think so, Taggar. I think it was you."

"That's enough, Lawton!" Rage, whether real or assumed, suffused Taggar's features, turning them dark and menacing in the dim light. "No man accuses me like that. Not even you."

"Oh, I'm not through yet." Steve kept his eyes on the other man, watching the whole of him, not just the eyes or the hands. "Somebody had to hire Starr for this job. He and his men don't work for free. Somebody had to tell him about the map and about our destination. He was here waiting for us. Don Carlos and his wards were newcomers to Guthrie. They wouldn't have known who Starr was or how to go about hiring him. It took someone with knowledge of the map and knowledge of Starr and his methods. That adds up to you. And there's more. You need the money to finance your political ambitions. Remember what you said about buying votes? How many votes would the gold buy? Enough, I'd guess, to get you elected governor."

"That's preposterous!" Taggar yelled. "I'm president and chief stockholder of a bank. I have all the funds I could use. I told you that too!"

Steve shook his head. "I don't think so. Any bank whose president and chief stockholder makes it a practice to lend money for ventures like treasure hunts can't be in good shape. I think your bank is failing and you're desperate for funds to bail it out and to finance your political career. Don Carlos and his wards, with their treasure map, must have looked like the perfect answer for you, provided you could get your hands on the gold without them around to make a legitimate claim to ownership. So you planned a double cross from the very beginning. That's where Joe Starr came in. You hired him to dog our trail and kill us when he had the chance. In fact, that first day I met with you and Carlos, I saw Starr coming from the direction of the bank. You had probably just finished a meeting with him. The fight Bruiser picked with Ramon was no coincidence. Starr saw a chance to get rid of one of us early on and took advantage of it. You hired me to make the whole thing look legitimate. You could come back to town as the sole, heroic survivor of an attack by unknown brigands."

"You can't prove any of this." Taggar's assumed anger had been replaced by a cold, shrewd cunning that could be seen in the hard, calculating glint in his eyes, the grim set of his mouth. This time, Steve thought, the emotion was genuine. He continued:

"It'll be easy enough to check on the condition of the bank once we get back to Guthrie. An audit should reveal what kind of shape it's in. And Starr won't be that hard to run to ground. He'll throw you over faster than those twins of his can draw their guns. He won't back you up, Taggar, not for a minute. His loyalty won't last beyond the threat of a prison sentence. You can bet on it. And Heck Thomas will be glad to cooperate in bringing you down, once I explain what you've tried to do."

"I still say you're crazy—" Taggar began. But even as he spoke he was spinning, bending to reach for the Winchester against the rock.

Steve skipped forward and kicked, snapping his foot up hard to meet Taggar's descending chest. The banker grunted, the impact straightening him, spinning him halfway around. He caught his balance, grabbing for his Colt.

Steve's gun was already out. Taggar froze, hand poised, as he saw it leveled dead at his chest.

"Thanks," Steve said tightly. "That saved us the trouble of an audit, Taggar." His eyes were hard. "If you want to make it even easier, go ahead and make your play."

Slowly Taggar relaxed, spreading his hands out well away from the butt of his holstered Colt. "No, I don't think so," he said thoughtfully. "Not against you."

"Drop it then."

Taggar complied. He took his eyes off Steve to glance out into the darkness.

"You were hoping to meet up with Starr and his boys when you went out there, weren't you?" Steve prodded. "That's why you volunteered for guard duty and offered to follow them earlier."

Taggar drew a deep, resigned breath. "Yeah," he admitted tiredly. "I still thought we might pull it off. Starr's a fool. We could have had you on that first try if he hadn't hired a bunch of greenhorns."

Steve saw that Ramon had joined the group. With the advent of darkness the young Spaniard must have relinquished his post on the ledge. Steve wondered how long Ramon had been listening.

"You've got it pretty much right," Taggar said. "The bank's about to fold. I needed a source of funds to keep it open and to finance my campaign when statehood comes. The gold would have been perfect. Why, with that kind of backing I could make it to the White House!"

"I don't know if the voters either here in the territory or in the rest of the country are as stupid as you seem to think," Steve said. "But you'll never have the chance to prove me wrong. Starr and his crew are long gone."

"You're wrong there, Lawton. Drop the gun!" The familiar voice crashed out of the darkness. Steve felt a tingling dread envelop him. He stood frozen, aware of the startled eyes of Felicia and the others on him.

"We've got five guns on you." Joe Starr's arrogant tones rolled once more out of the darkness. "Drop all the guns or we'll kill the whole bunch of you where you stand."

They made perfectly silhouetted targets against the fire at the back of the hollow, Steve thought. One gun or five made no difference. If they resisted, some of them would die. He let the Colt fall from his hand, heard the clatter as Alejandro and the others followed suit. Steve realized that he had made what was probably a fatal mistake for them all. Joe Starr and his men had not left the canyon, after all. They had only waited for the cover of night to return.

His guess was correct, he saw, as the five figures emerged from the darkness. In the lead was Starr himself, sneer confidently in place. Bulking huge at his side came Bruiser Jackson, the rifle in his hands looking like a toy. The third man was the stranger Steve had glimpsed when they had ridden by that afternoon. He had the hard-bitten mouth and cocky demeanor of a typical frontier hard case. In his years as a Ranger, Steve had seen his kind from one end of Texas to another, a cheap hired gun, but dangerous nonetheless.

A chill touched him as he saw the two pale figures who came forth last out of the darkness. Moving in eerie unison, still clad in their light buckskins, Simon and Luther Meade almost seemed to float forward like manifestations of the dark spirits Velador had described. They stopped side by side with uncanny precision, taking up a position just to the side of the hollow's entrance, where they could effectively cover the entire cut in their field of fire. Neither of them carried a rifle, but their hands hovered near the butts of their pearl-handled .45's. Their angelic faces were serene.

At Starr's command Bruiser collected the discarded guns. Taggar retrieved his own and then spoke in low tones with Starr for a moment. Then he addressed Steve. "The tables turn, don't they?" he said. "Joe has got some ideas about what to do with you. There's really not much I can do about it at this point."

"He'll turn on you once he has the gold," Steve warned grimly. "You're a fool if you don't see that." He knew his efforts were futile. Taggar had already burned too many of his bridges to go back now.

Predictably, Taggar only shrugged. "That's my worry, isn't it? You've got enough to concern you without taking on my problems. Besides, Joe and I have an understanding. I'll always have a place for someone with his particular talents, no matter how far I go. It's in both of our best interests to keep on working together."

Steve didn't argue further. Whether or not Taggar really believed what he said was irrelevant to Steve and his companions. Steve doubted that any of them would be alive to see the outcome of the relationship between Taggar and the gunman.

Starr strutted forward. "Things are a little different now, aren't they, Mr. High and Mighty Texas Ranger?" He shoved his face close to Steve's as he spoke.

Steve didn't reply. He had no chance against these odds. Taggar had been right. The tables had turned.

Starr was just beginning. "You know, I've never liked you, Lawton." He stalked back and forth in front of Steve as he spoke. "You, with your rep as a fast gun and your churchgoing ways. I was real happy when Mr. Taggar here hired me. But when I found out you were part of the deal, I would've almost been willing to take the job on for free. And this pretty filly—" He strutted over to Felicia, who lifted her head proudly and refused to meet his eye. "She's icing on the cake. The real, sweet kind, if you know what I mean. And I'll bet you do, Lawton. I'll bet you've had a little taste of this yourself."

He reached a grasping hand toward her. Ramon made a strangled sound and started forward. From where he stood nearby, Bruiser took a single step, interposing his bulk in front of Ramon. The young man halted, fists clenched. Starr snorted.

"Forget it, Ramon," Steve advised, making his voice as casual as possible. He wanted to draw the attention back to himself. "Starr won't do anything to anybody while I'm still alive. Even with me under the gun, he's scared of what I might do."

Starr pivoted sharply toward him, his face contorted. Steve wondered if he had succeeded too well. Starr was perfectly capable of shooting him where he stood.

"I ought to kill you right now," Starr snarled. He pulled his gun from its holster, clicked its hammer back, and shoved its barrel to within an inch of Steve's face. Steve heard Felicia's smothered gasp. He forced his eyes away from that looming barrel and met Starr's gaze levelly.

"It would be too easy, Lawton." The hammer clicked down under his thumb, the gun sliding smoothly back into its holster. "You beat up one of my boys in Guthrie. I said then that the score had to be evened. I think the time has come." He turned his head quickly toward Simon and Luther Meade. "How does that sound to you, boys?"

"We're ready, Mr. Starr," Luther said in a lilting voice.

"Hear that?" Starr had rounded on Steve once more.

"I promised the twins here a chance against you. They were real hurt when your pal Thomas spoiled things back in Guthrie. They've been wanting another opportunity ever since then. Isn't that right, boys?"

"That's right, Mr. Starr," Simon said. His voice was indistinguishable from his brother's.

"It shouldn't be much of a contest," Steve remarked drily. "I don't have a gun."

Starr curled his mouth scornfully. "We'll give you a gun," he said. "Not that it'll make any difference. I've seen my boys in action, Lawton. Gun or not, I think you're going down."

"Two to one are still long odds," Steve said.

Starr only shook his head. "I'm sorry, but Simon and Luther only work together. I told you they were joined arm-to-arm when they were born. And even though the doctors separated them, it's kind of like they're still joined mentally or something."

To one side Bruiser shifted his bulk with apparent impatience. Starr noticed the movement and flung a grin at the huge man. He looked back at Steve, his nostrils flaring eagerly. "After the twins dispose of you, I told Bruiser he could finish his job on the kid there."

"He might have his hands full this time," Steve said.

Starr laughed with seemingly genuine amusement, then sobered with frightening abruptness. His face became ugly. "You aren't in any position to be telling jokes!" he said savagely. "Simon! Luther!"

Like synchronized automatons the twins stepped forward, placing themselves some ten feet in front of Steve. Their eyes narrowed, and their lips parted with evil anticipation.

Starr retrieved Steve's Colt. He weighed it a moment

musingly. "You don't go in for fancy shooting irons do
you, Lawton?" he said contemptuously. "I've waited for
this." His tone had gone as ugly as his face. "I told you
back in Guthrie that I'd give you a choice someday. Remember that? Well, here's your choice—either take this
gun and go against the twins or I'll shoot you down where
you stand. Do you like your choice, Lawton? What'll it
be?"

Wordlessly Steve extended his hand for the gun.

Starr chuckled in triumph. "Raise your hands," he ordered. "I'll put it in the holster. We want this all even."

Steve complied and felt his holster sag with the familiar
weight. He wished he could check it, but he knew that his
first movement toward it would trigger the twins into action.

They were poised expectantly before him, their expressions feral and eager. Starr had withdrawn to stand almost
beside them. His expression was as eager as theirs. Bruiser
and the hard case were on the other side of the twins,
watching raptly. Taggar, a silent spectator, stood almost
outside the hollow. The members of Steve's party stood
together on Steve's right.

Steve looked back at the twins. He noted the tension
tightening the stances of their slender bodies. He had his
gun back, but to use it in any way except against the twins
would be suicide. They would cut him down in an instant
even if he could get a shot into Starr first. A grin twisted
Starr's face; he saw and understood Steve's dilemma.

Steve knew he had never really had any choice at all.
He lowered his hand until it hovered over the butt of the
.45.

*   *   *

There was a trick to this, Steve thought, a trick to taking on two gunmen at once in a stand-up fight. But it all depended on just how good Simon and Luther really were. If your opponents were fast enough and accurate enough, then all the techniques in the world wouldn't save your life.

They stood so closely together that their free hands brushed. Luther, the right-handed one, was on Steve's left. Left-handed Simon was to Steve's right. It seemed to him in that moment that they bared their teeth at him and hissed like dreadful demons.

Steve went for his gun. He had no compunctions about drawing first, not under these circumstances and not against these two killers. He drew, using wrist and hand to snap the .45 up out of the holster. At the same time he swung his left foot back in an arc, turning his body so that only his right side was presented to his opponents. He was aware of the .45 seeming to spring to his hand, aware of the simultaneous blurred movements as the twins drew with exactly matching speed that brought their .45's flashing up.

Steve fired as his barrel came level, the blast of Simon's left-handed gun merging with his in a single stuttering roar. Something went past his ear with a crack of displaced air. In that same instant Steve turned his gunhand palm down as he shifted it sideways. The barrel rotated with the move, coming into line with Luther on his left. Steve had offered only his right side to the twins so that Luther, on his left, drawing right-handed, would have to swing his gun a few crucial degrees farther across his body to bring it into line. Again the shots seemed to merge. This time something punched hard past Steve's chest.

Both twins were hammered backward, Simon starting

to go down first. As they fell Steve had a brief glimpse of
Joe Starr's stunned expression, reflex dropping the outlaw
leader's hand toward his holstered gun. Before the gun
could clear leather Steve shot him square in the chest.

Pivoting to his right Steve saw a blur of action. He saw
Ramon bend, his hand flashing to his boot. As he straightened, his arm lifted, went back past his head, then snapped
forward. The throwing knife, overlooked in his boot
sheath, winked in the firelight as it spun to bury itself in
Bruiser's Jackson's middle before the big man could fum-
ble his Winchester into play.

The last hard case stood for a moment, stunned. Alejandro dived for the big-game rifle where Jackson had set it
with the other weapons. Belatedly, the hard case grabbed
for his gun. Alejandro had the heavy rifle in his hands by
then, twisting up onto one knee, firing from the hip. The
rifle sounded like a cannon in the enclosed space. Its effect
on the hard case was almost as devastating, blasting him
back off his feet.

"Taggar!" Ramon cried. "He's escaping!"

Steve pivoted to see the banker dash out of sight into
the darkness. Taggar had made no effort to join the fight.

Bruiser Jackson lay where he had fallen, curled slightly.
The twins sprawled, unmoving. It looked almost as if their
free hands were reaching to grasp each other. Beside them
lay Joe Starr, his expression in death one of stupefied surprise.

"Stay here!" Steve snapped before anyone could speak.
"I'm going after Taggar."

Darting out of the hollow, he was careful not to silhou-
ette himself against the fire. Taggar was still armed and
still dangerous.

A faint crackling of limbs, the sound of a body forcing

itself through the underbrush, drew him. Taggar had taken to cover. In his first moments of flight he was making no effort to move silently. Steve darted past the pond to the beginnings of the growth, slowing as he drew near. He paused to listen. Only the sound of his own panting breath reached his ears. Taggar had gone to ground.

Immediately Steve threw himself flat. A gun cracked from somewhere in the brush, the bullet snapping overhead. Yes, Taggar was still dangerous. He had ceased his initial headlong flight and waited for a shot at his pursuer.

On his belly, Steve replaced the spent cartridges in his Colt. He snaked into the undergrowth, angling away from his point of entrance. Then he came cautiously to one knee. The small forest had taken on an eerie quality in the pale moonlight filtering through its skeletal branches. Brush cracked faintly in front of him and to his right. Steve felt a grim satisfaction. Either Sid Taggar had never learned how to move silently in the underbrush in his younger days or the years spent behind his desk at the bank had robbed him of the skill.

The sound stopped almost instantly. Steve eased forward on hands and knees. His own skills had not been eroded by years of office work. He felt rough stone under one palm, and realized that he was among the ancient ruins. His hand was resting on the foundation of one of the buildings.

The cry of fright and pain burst out of the darkness ahead of him. There was a frantic thrashing of brush and then silence.

Steve came to his feet and glided swiftly forward, gun in hand. Something silent and deadly had taken Taggar there among the ancient ruins.

He froze as a figure seemed to rise out of the ground

before him. Pale, broken moonlight shone on a gnarled muscular torso. Teeth gleamed in a weathered ancient face beneath a mane of silver hair. A bony fist gripped a great knife with the blade smeared black.

"Velador!" Steve gasped the name in startled recognition.

The figure vanished as if swallowed up by the night that had spawned it. Steve took two steps forward. His eyes probed the brush. His ears strained for sound. But there was nothing. He might almost have imagined that figure with its eerie spectral grin and the bowie knife that dripped blood black in the moonlight.

Then his foot hit something that yielded with an old and awful familiarity. He knew he had not imagined Velador's presence.

Taggar's pale face stared lifelessly up at him when he turned the still form over. Velador's battered old bowie had done the job well. Steve wondered what Taggar had thought in those last minutes. Had he known who or what it was that had risen out of the darkness to claim him?

Steve straightened and backed away from the body. He fought the urge to turn and run from this place of ancient ruins and ghastly death. Was Velador still watching?

"Velador." He spoke the name softly and then in a normal tone. His voice sounded loud and out of place.

Only the silence of the ruins and the brush answered him. He holstered his gun. "Thank you, my friend," he said into the night.

Somewhere an owl hooted, the sound rising and falling. An owl—bird of evil omen, according to the Indians.

Steve turned and walked back through the underbrush. The owl called again, but he did not look behind him. He asked himself if Taggar had been as poor a woodsman as he had supposed, or if that last broken branch had been only a ruse to lure him into range of the man's gun. Had Taggar been waiting in silent ambush? Had Velador in fact saved Steve's life? In those moments when he had seen the old brave rising from his kill only to disappear into the brush, Velador had not moved like a cripple at all.

Alejandro and Ramon had put the dead outside the hollow by the time Steve returned. Steve did not look at the still shapes. They would have to be buried tomorrow, as would Taggar. Seven men dead, including the sniper, he thought ruefully. But if they had not died, then innocent people would have suffered and died at their hands instead.

Alejandro waited at the mouth of the cut. Even in the darkness Steve could detect that hard glitter in his eyes. The Spaniard held the big rifle tightly in his grip.

"You were superb, Stephen!" Alejandro greeted him. "Two against one, and you killed them both, then shot down their leader before he could draw! I got one and Ramon used his knife on the big one!"

Steve swallowed hard, but the bitterness would not leave his mouth. Alejandro was studying him with a cold dispassion despite the excitement of his greeting.

"And what of Taggar?" Alejandro asked.

"Dead," Steve answered. "Velador killed him."

"Velador? The old Indian?"

Steve nodded and walked on into the draw. He drank from one of the canteens, then related what had happened out in the underbrush.

"But why did Velador kill him?" Felicia wondered aloud later when the two of them sat by the fire.

Steve shook his head. "Maybe to save my life. I don't know."

Her lovely features were troubled. "He seemed so old and helpless and frail that night when he came to our camp. He did not seem as though he would kill like that."

"He's not as old or helpless as he looks." Steve remembered vividly the ease with which Velador had eluded him. "But I've never heard of him killing anyone or even being blamed for a killing."

"It is sad that he must live out here in these mountains alone."

Somehow Steve had never thought of the loneliness that the old man must endure in his solitary existence. "He doesn't have anywhere else to go. He'd die on a reservation. He has his memories, his dreams of the past."

Felicia shook her head sadly. "It is not enough. He must be terribly, terribly lonely. And sad."

Steve turned his gaze toward Ramon, who approached the fire where they sat. Felicia had earlier offered to cook, but none of them had been hungry. Steve felt only a deep weariness that weighed heavily upon him. Alejandro, by contrast, seemed possessed of a nervous, driving energy. He prowled the hollow with feline intensity.

"You did well, Ramon," Steve told the younger man.

"I remembered what you told me," Ramon said. "I was scared, but I knew we must fight or they would kill us. I did what I had to do. But—" He looked almost pleadingly at Steve.

"But what?"

"There is nothing noble or uplifting in killing a man," Ramon said softly. "Not even one such as Bruiser Jackson."

"That's the final lesson you had to learn," Steve said

with compassion. "Some men never learn it. Sometimes killing is justifiable, like it was tonight, but it's never noble or enriching."

Ramon inclined his head toward the front of the hollow where Alejandro prowled on restless guard. "Carlos seems to have enjoyed it, as if killing that man was somehow more to him than food or drink. I do not like what I saw in his eyes."

"Be certain that it never comes to your eyes," Steve advised.

"And Taggar would have killed us all."

"For the gold. And the power it could give him."

"How did you know?" Felicia laid a hand on his arm.

"I guessed," Steve admitted. "When Starr mentioned the map, I knew one of us had to have hired him. Taggar had the motive and the opportunity, which neither of you nor Don Carlos had. When I confronted him, he broke and tried for his Winchester. That was the final proof."

"All this time he planned to betray us. You saved us, Steve."

"Ramon helped," Steve said. "And Carlos."

"She is right," Ramon said. "You saved us. I would not have been able to act if not for what you had told me. You have been a good teacher. My thanks." Ramon rose and moved away.

Steve watched him go. "He's a good man," he said to Felicia.

"Now he is a man," she agreed. "Not so many days ago he was a boy. He is right. You have taught him well."

"He would have turned out all right given some time. I just helped him along a little."

"No, you did much more than that. You gave him an example of how to be a man. It is something he has never really had." Her face grew troubled, as if some thought related to her words had disturbed her.

"What's wrong?"

"Is it that you can read my mind?" she asked. "Do you know my thoughts?"

"You looked disturbed."

She glanced toward the front of the draw. Her voice was low as she spoke. "Carlos says that tomorrow we will find the gold."

"And that disturbs you?"

"It shouldn't, should it?" she said. "I should be excited and glad. It is strange that I am not."

"Gold or money doesn't always solve all our problems. It makes some worse and even creates new ones. And there are more important things than gold." *Things like the love of a beautiful and virtuous woman,* he thought. But he did not speak the words aloud.

Felicia drew her knees up and wrapped her arms around them. "Maybe Velador was right. Maybe we shouldn't try to find the gold at all. Maybe we should just leave it alone."

"Carlos would never agree to that after coming this far."

"It is *our* map!" she cried. "Mine and Ramon's! It does not belong to Carlos. He has no claim to it except through Ramon and me!" Then she slumped, and the fire went out of her. "But you are right. He would never give up now that we are so close," she went on dispiritedly. "And finding the gold would not change things. He would still be our guardian. He would want to marry me even more, so that he would have a better claim to the gold." A shudder rippled over her.

"I'll see that he leaves you alone," Steve promised.

"Once you're of age, you can become Ramon's guardian until he's an adult. You'll be wealthy. Carlos won't be able to harm you."

There were other things that he wanted to say. But he did not. If they found the gold, she would be fabulously wealthy. Undoubtedly she would return to the life of an aristocrat in Spain. Once that happened, she would most likely laugh at any offer to be the wife of a rancher with only a few head of cattle and some big dreams. But for now he could keep this promise to her.

Her fingers touched his hand. "Now you are troubled. What is wrong?"

"Nothing," he said. "Don't worry about Carlos." Her eyes still questioned him. To evade them he asked, "Where is the gold from here? Do you know?"

"It is back toward the mouth of the canyon."

"Back the way we came?" Steve asked in surprise.

She nodded confirmation. "The distance can only be calculated from the ruins. That is why we had to locate them first."

So they had already passed the gold, Steve mused. Somewhere back along the canyon was the entrance to the cave where the Indians had concealed the gold.

A shadow fell across them. Felicia gasped, and Steve looked up at Alejandro, who had approached with the silence of a hunter. The Spaniard held his huge rifle cradled in his arms. His eyes glittered down at them.

"I will take the first watch, Stephen," he said. "I will not be able to sleep. I feel the nearness of the gold. It is exhilarating, like a tonic, an elixir that makes my blood race in me. Tomorrow, when we find the gold, will be the climax of my plans and efforts." He gazed hungrily down at Felicia. "Are you not eager, my dear?"

She looked away and did not answer.

Alejandro grinned at Steve as one man to another. "Perhaps the excitement has been too much for her, eh, Stephen? Women are like that. They cannot understand the thrill of the hunt or the gunfight. Tonight, when we matched our skills with weapons against those of other men, was very stimulating, was it not, Stephen? More exciting than the hunt. Now I understand the allure your trade holds for you."

"It's not my trade. I don't kill men for money."

"But you hunt them."

Steve was too tired for this pointless debate. "I track down wanted men. And when I do, I'm acting as a U.S. deputy marshal. There's a difference." He rose and offered a hand to Felicia. "But you're right. It would be a good idea to post a guard. You're welcome to the first shift. I think the rest of us should turn in."

"As you say, Stephen."

Steve watched Alejandro move away. He felt Felicia draw instinctively closer to him.

Chapter Thirteen

"But there is no cave. There is nothing here at all!"
Felicia's voice carried the same bewilderment that Steve
himself felt.

The four of them stood before the empty expanse of canyon wall. Only a few hardy shrubs clung to the bare granite rock. Boulders were strewn along the base of the wall.
Higher up, Steve could see a clump of brush clinging to
a ledge. But nowhere was there any sign of the mouth of
a cave.

Alejandro stood silently, staring at the canyon wall as
if he might penetrate its secrets by the force of his gaze
alone. His handsome features expressed a dismayed frustration. Felicia stood next to Steve. Ramon was a little to
one side.

Steve looked down the canyon. Not too far from here
was the spot where he had confronted Zeke Spurd. And
beyond that was the mouth of the canyon. Alejandro, following the directions in the map and the journal, had led
them in the early afternoon hours to this baffling length
of wall.

Steve went closer to the granite face. He himself had
passed this spot more than once over the years. Never had

he given it more than cursory attention. But now as he stared at it, he wanted to blink and refocus his eyes. It seemed that the light was playing some trick of perspective on him.

He moved still closer, only vaguely conscious of the others watching him. The cave mouth was supposedly concealed somehow, he recalled. Yet it seemed impossible for anything to be concealed in this naked granite wall. But there was still a troubling misalignment of light and shadow that teased his eye.

At above ground level where he had been looking, the stone was broken by what he at first took to be a scar of some kind. He pressed himself against the unyielding rock, peering up at an awkward angle. Impossibly, some three feet up the wall, was a tall narrow slit of blackness. Steve realized that he was staring into a narrow cleft in the wall, concealed by a curtain of stone from any but the closest examination. Unless viewed from this angle, the cleft would be virtually invisible.

"Get the lanterns," Steve ordered. He stepped back from the wall and, magically, the black slit seemed to disappear. The natural contours of the stone had provided an almost flawless camouflage to the cave entrance. It was no wonder the Indians had chosen this as their hiding place, and no wonder that it had escaped the detection of gold seekers down through the centuries. Even with the map to pinpoint its location, they had almost missed it.

He pulled himself up into the cleft, feeling the brush of cool damp air that bespoke a large cavern. Felicia passed him up a lighted lantern. In moments Alejandro joined him. With Steve in the lead and the others pressing close behind, they entered the cave.

The cleft was tight and narrow. No ancient craftsmen

had labored to alter the natural contours of the stone here. Steve squeezed past out-thrusting teeth of stone. The disturbing image formed in his mind of the four of them trying to slip between the fangs and into the maw of some gigantic, slumbering beast.

They found themselves in a room-sized chamber with a floor of sand. Steve lifted the lantern high. Ramon, also carrying one, did likewise. The black mouth of a tunnel confronted them across the chamber. The sand along the walls was littered with stone fragments and the trails of small mammals and reptiles that must use this place as a den. But the center of the chamber was clear of such tracks.

Alejandro stepped forward impatiently. Steve thrust an arm to block him. "Wait."

"What?" Alejandro demanded. But he made no move to bypass Steve's extended arm.

Steve frowned. Was it only his imagination coupled with the indistinct light, or did the center of the chamber's floor appear to sag ever so slightly? A fragment of stone the size of his two fists lay at his feet. He scooped it up and tossed it into the center of the chamber. Immediately the floor collapsed, falling away on either side to reveal a gaping hole in the center of the chamber. A pit trap. Steve's instincts had been correct; the Indians had not left the gold unguarded.

"How did you know?" Felicia asked.

"There were no tracks on the sand over the pit," Steve told her. Something about the implications of his answer troubled him, but he took no time to analyze it.

Together he and Alejandro edged forward. The Spaniard uttered a muffled oath as they stared down into the pit. Sharpened wooden stakes rose up from the pit's floor.

Scattered among them were bones that gleamed palely in the light. Steve spotted a staring human skull. The pit's last victim had never been removed. Sometime in the past, a seeker had discovered the entrance and died here alone.

They skirted the pit, averting their eyes from its grisly contents. Steve felt the tension trembling in Alejandro beside him. An answering eagerness rose up in him as well. He forced himself to caution. But the lure of what might lie back in the cave drew him with magnetic compulsion.

At the head-high mouth of the tunnel he extended the lantern cautiously in front of them, eyes searching the darkness. Where there had been one trap, there might well be more.

"There," Alejandro said hoarsely. "A trip wire."

Steve lowered the lantern and detected the thin line stretched taut across the passageway. Alejandro, with the instincts of a hunter, had spotted it.

"Stand back," Steve ordered, and he drew his bowie. Moving back, he lifted the heavy knife, took aim, and threw it. The gleaming blade severed the line and struck sparks as it rebounded from the stone floor. There was a rush of air. Felicia gasped and caught Steve's arm. The heavy tree trunk that swung down out of the darkness, released by the severed line, was sharpened to a deadly point. Anyone stepping on the line, or breaking it in passing, would have been directly in the path of the massive, sharpened log swinging down to impale him.

Steve retrieved the bowie and slashed at the ropes suspending the sharpened log like a barrier across their way. It crashed to the floor. From somewhere in the darkness ahead came a dry whirring sound, as of pebbles being shaken together. Steve swallowed. He knew that sound. But it was louder than he had ever heard it.

Waving the others back, he stepped into the tunnel. He noted dimly that it had been smoothed and widened by human effort. Something moved sinuously in the shadows on the floor ahead.

Steve reached for his Colt, then hesitated. He had no idea what effect a shot and its echoes might have on the structure of this place. Once more he drew his knife. The movement seemed to trigger a renewed burst of the ominous clatter. The cave no longer felt cool to him. Sweat beaded on him. Slowly he extended the lantern to arm's length and stared into the shadows cloaking the floor.

A triangular reptilian head, larger than his open hand, lifted toward him, forked black tongue flicking. Massive scaly coils shifted, and the tail beat the floor in a frenzy. Steve swallowed in a dry throat. He recalled the enormous rattlesnake he had seen the day before in the canyon. This one was even larger, a gigantic mound of shifting, heaving coils that lay directly in their path and all but filled the width of the passage.

Steve heard a sharply indrawn breath at his shoulder. He realized that Alejandro had eased forward to stand beside him. The snake's great blunt head lifted higher, level with Steve's waist, tongue licking the air. Alejandro moved as if to unsling his rifle from where he carried it over his shoulder.

Abruptly, as if that movement, added to the two men's presence, was the final irritant, the snake lowered its head. Its scaled body shifted and uncoiled. In a blur of movement it darted into the black mouth of a narrow crevice. Its whole scaled length writhed from sight within seconds.

Steve exhaled sharply. Somehow, he suspected, perhaps with live prey to lure it, the huge serpent had been induced to make its den here, to act as a living guardian for this cave and its contents. But the presence of the two men had been too much for the reptile. Nonaggressive by nature unless hunting or cornered, it had fled to the safety of some impenetrable lair deep in the stone walls.

Steve stared after the snake. The stray thought that had disturbed him about the pit trap suddenly crystallized in his mind. The presence of the snake, the functional tripwire, the meticulously reset pit trap were not the work of Indians long dead.

"¡Basta!" Alejandro exclaimed. "Enough!" He snatched the lantern from Steve and strode forward. Steve tensed. But no trap doors opened beneath Alejandro's feet. No sharpened logs swung down to impale him. And in the light of his lantern Steve could see that the passage broadened out into a larger chamber. At the mouth of that chamber, lantern uplifted, Alejandro stopped dead, as if he had come unexpectedly to the end of some limiting tether. Tawny reflections cast back the flickering light of the lantern.

Steve went forward. He peered past Alejandro's motionless form. He felt the breath catch in his throat.

Fifty burro-loads of solid gold ingots, the legends had said. Enough to be set in waist-high stacks that ran for more than twenty feet along the wall of the cavern chamber, glinting with burnished fire under the lantern's glow.

Alejandro took a single step toward those yellow piles. The others crowded in behind him, caught in that moment by the irresistible lure of the yellow ingots. And it was Alejandro who finally moved. He took another step forward and then another until he could reach out a trembling hand to caress the nearest stack of gold bars.

Steve moved forward and took one in his hand. He was surprised at its weight, at the warmth that he imagined emanated from it. The brick in his hand seemed to draw his eyes and hold them. He was only vaguely aware of Felicia and Ramon raptly surveying the piles of ingots.

At last Steve set the ingot back into place. The gold was here. It was real. Even believing the map and the journal, he had doubted that they would ever stand here in the presence of the ancient treasure.

He shook his head to clear it. The glow of the gold was mesmerizing. It dulled the mind and sense to all except its seductive presence. Alejandro had moved off a little distance, still brushing his hands over the smooth surfaces of the stacked ingots.

Felicia turned to Steve, smiling, her face as radiant as the glow of the gold. Her misgivings were apparently forgotten in the excitement of actually finding the treasure. Steve returned her hug. He turned his head so that he could continue to watch Alejandro. Thus he saw the moment when Alejandro seemed to stiffen, as if, like Steve, forcing himself back to reality.

Felicia turned to the gold, still absorbed by it. Steve saw Alejandro glance in their direction, then look back at the gold. His posture was stiff and strained.

"I'd better go check on the horses," Steve said. "We didn't tie them too securely when we came in here." There was little reaction to his words.

He turned to go, and in turning touched Ramon's shoulder lightly. Ramon looked around. His face wore the same bemused expression that Steve guessed his own must have worn in those first few, breathtaking moments. Surreptitiously he squeezed Ramon's forearm hard, and saw some of the bemusement fade. "Five minutes." Steve mouthed the words. "Cover me."

He went quickly on, berating himself almost immediately for the way he was handling this. Ramon's recent maturity notwithstanding, he was trusting his life to an inexperienced ally who, hypnotized by the great hoard of gold, might not have even understood his terse, whispered instructions. But he had to play it out this way. Relying on Ramon was just another element of the risk he ran.

He saw no sign of the giant rattlesnake and hoped that it still remained in its lair. He stepped over the sharpened log and skirted the pit. Squeezing through the narrow passage, he emerged into the sunlight. Its brilliance was blinding after the cave's dim interior. They had left the horses before the seemingly bare canyon wall. He moved them to a strip of growth against the far wall and began to hobble them so they could browse among the sparse vegetation.

He forced himself to work purposefully, sneaking only an occasional glance at the cave entrance. It was eerie; even knowing where the cave entrance was located, he had trouble detecting the spot. Once left behind, it seemed almost to have become invisible. He felt that he was safe as long as he was among the horses. Afterward, when he was in the clear, would be the time of greatest danger.

He hobbled Traveler last, lingering over the paint, taking the opportunity to study the canyon wall opposite. Still there was no sign. Perhaps he had been wrong. Resolutely he withdrew his Winchester from its sheath. Carrying it at his side, he walked back out into the open toward the concealed mouth of the cave.

He was gripping the rifle tightly, telling himself that with each step the danger lessened and the likelihood increased that he had been wrong. Still, he kept his eyes on the spot where he was certain the cave entrance lay.

A single flicker of movement to the right of that spot

was all the warning he had. His eyes darted instinctively to that point, just as the tall familiar figure stepped smoothly into view, seeming to materialize out of the canyon wall itself. He saw the big rifle come up with practiced ease. Steve was already flinging himself down as it belched its roaring flame. He realized that, after all, he had been right. But he had been watching the wrong spot, and he had been a fool to trust Ramon, because he was caught now in the open, helpless.

He rolled frantically across the stony ground, coming out of it on his belly, Winchester lining up for what he thought was a hopeless shot at the aiming figure. Another shape seemed to materialize out of the rock. It flung itself at the rifleman like a beast of prey. Steve stayed his pull of the Winchester's trigger as the two figures, locked in a grapple, toppled from the cave mouth the short distance to the canyon floor.

Steve was up and sprinting forward. He skidded to a halt, using his momentum to power the swinging foot he used to kick the big-game rifle away from Alejandro's reaching hand. Steve snapped the barrel of his Winchester down to point. "That's all!" he barked.

Don Carlos Alejandro slumped in defeat. Ramon crawled slowly erect from atop him. He stared at Steve with wide eyes. "I did not understand when you told me to cover you," he said in a rush. "But when I saw Carlos leave also, I knew what you wanted me to do. I followed him, but was too late. When he fired I sprang upon him."

Steve nodded in wordless acknowledgment. "Get up," he ordered Alejandro.

Alejandro climbed to his feet. He was trembling with rage and frustration. His gaze swung back and forth between Steve and Ramon. "You tricked me!" he gasped.

"I set a trap," Steve said. "That's something any good hunter knows how to do."

Steve led the way back into the gold chamber to escape the sun's heat. "I didn't know for sure," he said as he bound Alejandro's hands. "I didn't have the evidence like I did with Taggar telling Starr about the map. But I knew you, Don Carlos. I knew that bloodthirsty, hunter's nature of yours. And I knew how desperate you were for money and how ruthless you could be in getting what you want. Felicia had told me about some of your past business ventures, how you ruined her father, drove him to suicide, and then effectively seized control of his estate through his children. She also told me of your marriage proposal to her. A man who would do that wouldn't hesitate to double-cross and murder his own wards, much less a hired guide, to get his hands on this treasure." Steve gestured at the stacks of ingots.

"I had to give you a chance to betray yourself," he went on. "The only way to do that was to give you the perfect opportunity to kill me. I had to set a trap and use myself for bait. If I was right, then there was no way you'd pass up a chance like that."

Steve looked around. There was a kind of reassuring comfort in being within sight and touch of the gold.

Alejandro, his hands bound behind him, sat against one wall. His face was still savage as he confronted his captors. Ramon and Felicia had not lost the looks of stunned disbelief that revelation of their guardian's treachery had brought to their faces.

"How could you, Carlos?" Felicia asked. "How could you come all this way with us, all the while plotting and planning to murder us so that you could have the gold? You raised us like we were your own children!"

This time Alejandro responded. "You would have had a choice," he said with suppressed rage. "You could have still accepted my offer of marriage. I would have given you that opportunity. It wouldn't have been so bad being my wife with this treasure in our hands, would it?"

Felicia shuddered. "May God have mercy on your soul," she whispered fervently. "How could you think that I would ever have anything to do with you if you had killed Steve and Ramon?"

"That would have been your choice," Alejandro responded coldly. "This treasure could make many things bearable, particularly if your alternative was death."

Steve stared at the man. He was chilled by his absolute amorality. Like Taggar, Alejandro had planned only treachery. He had been lured by his greed to stalk his companions with the cold-blooded, merciless nature of the hunter.

"It was a mistake, hiring you, Lawton," Alejandro continued. "We needed you, but I knew that eventually you would mean trouble. Still, I couldn't afford to kill you sooner, not until we found the gold. You were too valuable to us. I've known of that map for years," he went on. "And I've always yearned to come over here after the treasure. Your father, Felicia, told me about the map. He even showed it to me. But he would never approve an expedition to find the treasure. He put too much stock in the oath your grandfather had demanded from him, and his father before him, all the way back to Captain Vendegas, curse him!"

"We should have honored the oath," Felicia said. "Even though we had never taken it."

"The oath was nonsense, the foolishness of a demented old man! This gold—any gold—is there for whoever is strong enough to take it and keep it as his own. I learned that in the world of finance. But I had too much to occupy me in overseeing my own affairs, as well as yours, in trying to recoup our losses, to worry about the map for a long time after your father's death. But then it became necessary to acquire more capital. I realized that soon you would be an adult. I knew I could not delay seeking the treasure any longer. Somehow I never doubted that we would be successful. I have always achieved success when the need was there. I knew that once we found the treasure, there would be no legitimate legal claimants if the two of you were dead, or if you, Felicia, were my wife. Either way there would have been no one to dispute my title to the gold.

"Felicia." His voice grew softer, and he stared imploringly, compellingly, up at her. "Think what it would mean for us to have this gold together, you and I, as husband and wife. I've wanted you for years, ever since you came back from school that summer. And you've known it. I've seen it in your eyes. Think about it! We can give Ramon a share, even pay Steve the bonus we promised. Back in Spain or anywhere else in the world, there would be no doors that would be closed to us with this kind of wealth. And you need me. You know that. You need me to look after you just like I have in the past. We can forget about this little episode. I was wrong and I admit it. It was all a mistake."

Felicia had begun to shake her head in denial. "Stop it!" she cried. "What you are saying is vile, horrible!"

Alejandro turned to Steve. "How about you, Stephen? How would half of this gold suit you? We'll dispose of these two and split it down the middle. No one would ever be the wiser. The bodies would never be found here. You could go anywhere, do anything, with this kind of fortune."

Steve felt contempt twist his mouth. "I told you once—I only work for my wages. There isn't enough gold here or anywhere else to get me to go along with you on any deal you ever dreamed of."

Alejandro's expression was one of profound disgust. He settled his shoulders back against the wall and glared defiantly.

"What do we do now?" Ramon asked.

"I've been thinking about it," Steve told him. "Felicia and I will take Don Carlos back to Guthrie and turn him over to Heck Thomas. We'll also take as much of the gold as we can carry on the horses and mules. You'll stay here and keep an eye on the gold. We'll come back with enough mules to haul it all out."

Ramon nodded thoughtfully. "It is a good plan." He glared at Alejandro contemptuously. "You should be hanged!"

"You may feel differently later," Steve cautioned. "Besides, what happens to him will be up to the law, not us."

Ramon drew a deep breath. "You are right, as usual," he said.

Steve clapped him on the shoulder. "Let's start getting some of this gold out. There's no point in waiting to start back. Don Carlos can even give us a hand carrying the gold."

Alejandro cursed them all roundly, but, in the end, hands bound in front of him, arms burdened with several of the heavy ingots, he preceded them out of the cave. Each of them, even Felicia, carried a load of the ingots. It was surprising, Steve thought, what a small fraction of the gold their combined burdens comprised. The value of the wealth represented by the entire treasure would be incredible.

Again he was all but blinded by the sunlight as he stepped down behind Alejandro, who was in the lead. Briefly he paused, blinking. As his eyes focused he both saw and heard the arrow take Alejandro precisely between the shoulder blades. It pitched him forward onto his face atop his load of golden ingots.

Steve pulled up short, halting himself in midstride, blocking Ramon and Felicia behind him. Alejandro lay motionless. He was dead. His spine had undoubtedly been severed by the arrow. It had been fired from above, from somewhere on the canyon wall over their heads. This close in, hugging the wall itself, Steve knew that he and his companions were safe for the moment. The angle was too steep to allow the archer a shot at them.

The archer. Steve stared at the unadorned arrow. He knew, with a grim chill, what he should have realized when he had seen the well-maintained traps in the cave.

He let the gold ingots fall from his arms. "Velador!" he called. The canyon walls bounced the name back to him in diminishing reverberations.

"I hear you, Cazador," the familiar voice rolled down from above in response.

"Why are you doing this?" Steve shouted.

"Because I must protect the gold. It is my duty, my oath to my people. I have guarded it for more years than I can remember. Your lives are forfeit now that you have seen it."

Steve sagged back against the hard granite. *Velador,* he thought. *The Watcher. Guardian of the lost treasure of Devil's Canyon.* He should have known. The tales of lost and missing men, the rumors of something dangerous and evil in the canyon, even the canyon's name itself—all pointed to the presence of some mysterious and formidable protector watching over the canyon and its secrets.

How many men over the years, he wondered numbly, had fallen to the redoubtable old warrior lurking among the barren crags of these mountains? How many men like Alejandro and Taggar had given their lives in search of the gold? He thought of the nameless skeleton back in the pit, of the stories he had mentioned to Felicia. Perhaps Velador had been right, after all. Perhaps there were spirits haunting this canyon, the spirits of those who died by his ancient hand.

"You and I are friends, Velador," he called out.

"No longer, Cazador!" The Indian's voice seemed to speak out of the air itself. "You betrayed that friendship when you came seeking the canyon's secrets, searching for the gold. I cannot let you live now."

So here was the final treachery, Steve thought, the final double cross of Devil's Canyon. But was Velador the treacherous one or, as the Indian asserted, was he himself the betrayer, the double crosser? Velador's actions were not born out of greed but out of loyalty to a cause, dedication to his people and their vanished ways. And what, Steve asked himself, had been his own motives in coming here? Money, of course. His wages. Whether he claimed a share in the treasure or not, it had been his own greed that had brought him here in defiance of Velador's warnings.

"I'm sorry, Velador." His voice echoed hollowly.

"As am I." Velador's disembodied tones came back to him. "But you have left me no choice."

"I cannot let you kill those who are with me."

"You cannot stop me, Cazador."

Steve slipped the .45 from its holster. There had been no way to determine Velador's precise location from the sound of his eerie, disembodied voice. But the old Indian had to be somewhere on the wall above them, safe from any shot from Steve, but also prevented from targeting them with his arrows. Velador would act swiftly to remedy that. Or would he? Might not the old brave simply remain where he was and wait for his chance?

Steve licked dry lips. It made no difference. He could not stay here and wait for Velador to kill them. And of the Indian's ability to do just that he had no doubt. Alejandro's motionless form bore testimony to Velador's capability and willingness to kill.

Turning, Steve motioned Ramon and Felicia to the cover of the boulders scattered along the base of the wall. They had not explored the cave. Taking cover in it would be a greenhorn's move. There was no way of knowing what secret tunnels, what obscure passages, might give Velador access to it, enabling him to emerge at their backs.

Briefly he knelt there with them, whispering instructions. His eyes scanned their surroundings restlessly. "Stay here with Felicia," he ordered Ramon. "Don't argue with me. Velador's different from Taggar or Alejandro or even Starr and his men. If he gets me, he'll have to come here after you. Then you might get a shot at him. Believe me, that's your only chance. Understand?"

Ramon nodded. His face was set with grim determination.

Felicia reached toward Steve, her eyes wide and frightened. "What are you going to do?"

"I've got to go after him," Steve said. "If I can't stop him, he'll kill us all."

Chapter Fourteen

*D*own the canyon from their location, an arm of underbrush and scrub oak extended from the far wall across almost the full width of the canyon. From its cover, Steve
thought, if he could reach it, he would have a clear view
of the face of the wall against which they now crouched.
Once he spotted Velador, he would have a shot at him.

They had two rifles—Steve's Winchester and Alejandro's big-game piece. There was also Alejandro's foreign
handgun. Steve left them all with Ramon and Felicia, en-
suring that they would both be armed and have a spare
weapon as well. Their other rifles were with their horses
across the canyon. There was no way to reach them beneath the threat of Velador's archery.

Where was the Indian warrior? Still perched above
them, waiting for one of them to show himself as a target?
Or maneuvering to get a clear shot? Steve didn't know and
he could not afford to wait. He must carry the fight to his
opponent if they were to have any chance at all.

Colt in hand, he slipped along the base of the canyon
wall, pressing close to the granite. Once he looked back,
but an outward bulge of the wall had cut off his view of
Ramon and Felicia. They had become his wards, and he

their guardian. He looked up at the sheer wall looming above him. He was still safe as long as he stayed in close.

He reached the point of the wall opposite the extending arm of underbrush. Thirty feet of open ground separated him from it, thirty feet that he would have to cross. But Velador, presumably perched somewhere above with that entire stretch of the canyon to survey, would not be able to cover all of it simultaneously. By the time he spotted Steve in the open, if he spotted him at all, it would be too late to launch an arrow before Steve had reached cover.

The butt of the .45 was slick with sweat in Steve's grip. He shifted his hold but did not reholster the weapon. There was no point in waiting any longer, he told himself. With that thought he dashed out from the canyon wall. He swerved automatically as he ran, zigzagging by instinct and training.

The arrow ripped down across his forearm with a blow like a fist. The .45 dropped from his convulsed fingers. He flung himself across the last few yards as a second arrow went past him. He dived into the cover of the underbrush, thorns and branches tearing at him. He rolled sideways, and a third arrow sliced through the brush where he been. He writhed back deeper into cover and lay still.

No more arrows sought him for the moment. He realized numbly that Velador had gotten off three arrows during an interval in which many men could not have fired a handgun that many times. And—the realization struck him with a chill of despair—Velador had been waiting for him. Velador had known what he planned. There was no other explanation for the swift, uncanny accuracy of the arrows.

From his vantage point, Velador must have spotted the extending arm of growth and guessed that Steve would make for it to utilize its cover. Anticipating the move, Velador had simply shifted positions and waited for Steve to act. Only his zigzagging run had saved him from dying as Alejandro had died. Still, Velador had disarmed him. His .45 lay in the open, as out of reach as if it had been on the moon.

Steve examined his arm. The wound was like the shallow slash of a knife. The arm was not permanently damaged, but it would stiffen eventually. Steve bound it tightly with his kerchief. But bandaging himself was no more than a token gesture at delaying the inevitable. Armed only with his bowie, he had no chance against Velador's superior positioning, weaponry, and knowledge of the terrain.

He recalled Velador's uncanny ability to vanish among the rocks and draws of these mountains. He remembered the spectral vision of Velador rising from the body of his victim in the night. He remembered the agility of the brave's movements. They had not been the movements of an old man but, rather, those of a young and vigorous warrior in his prime. The old Indian's crippled shuffle and his stiff, awkward movements, Steve realized, had all been a sham, a trick to lull those like him into underestimating Velador's true abilities. Velador had allowed himself to be seen after killing Taggar. He had shown himself to Steve as part warning and part challenge. Otherwise he could have slipped away into the night unseen.

Steve lowered his face to the mat of twigs and leaves that carpeted the hard, stony ground. He had no chance against the ghostly, inhuman skills of the warrior. Velador knew this canyon as no man living. He would stalk Steve relentlessly to his death through its familiar mazes, as he must have stalked others down over the decades. When

Steve was dead, he would turn back for Ramon and Felicia. They would be helpless against him. Steve remembered the pale bones gleaming in the pit in the cave. Would their bones soon join those to lie forgotten in the Canyon of the Devil?

What had been his thought when Velador had helped him to track Zeke Spurd and then had disappeared among the rocks? He had been glad that it was not Velador he hunted among these ancient peaks. Now it was Velador who hunted him, as he himself had hunted Zeke Spurd, who had awaited him in ambush with the old Sharps.

Steve's mind froze. Slowly he lifted his face from the ground. What had become of that old buffalo gun? It had spun unfired from Spurd's hands at the impact of Steve's bullet, dropping from sight into the canyon. Had it dropped all the way to the canyon floor to be dashed to pieces? Or had it, maybe, lodged in the underbrush that choked so much of the canyon's floor?

Through the intervening tangle of growth, Steve peered up at the canyon wall where Velador undoubtedly lurked, awaiting another shot at his prey. He could see nothing of the warrior, but he knew that Velador was up there somewhere, waiting and watching.

Steve felt his teeth grind together. Slim it might be, but the Sharps offered him a chance. He would not lie here and wait helplessly for Velador to finish him off and then kill Ramon and Felicia.

The ledge from where Spurd had tried to ambush him was not far down the canyon from here. Stealthily, using every skill he had acquired over the years, Steve began to work his way farther back into the concealing brush.

Velador would know that he was unarmed and that he had gone to ground. The Indian warrior might expect him to try for the .45 or attempt to return to the cave. But he would not expect Steve to make for the site of his showdown with Spurd. Steve cast his mind back. He was certain he had not heard the Sharps discharge as it most likely would have done had it struck on stone. He had seen no signs of recent rainfall in the arid mountains, which might have fouled the charge or rusted the mechanism. If he could find the rifle, he might have a chance.

When he had writhed his way far back in the undergrowth to where he could catch only occasional glimpses of the far wall, he moved on hands and knees down the course of the canyon. He was careful not to disturb the growth so as to betray his presence to one watching from above. He stopped frequently to listen and watch. Screened by the branches, he peered intently at the wall, searching for some sign of his enemy. The area where Velador must be under cover was indented by numerous ledges and outcroppings of rock. He could see no sign of Velador, but he knew that meant nothing. In terrain such as this, the warrior would be like a phantom.

Steve began to make his way back toward the wall, scanning it now to locate the ledge on which Spurd had waited. Would he be able to identify it from this angle? He came to his feet, crouched, slipping silently through the underbrush like a phantom himself.

There, that was surely the ledge he sought. He stared up at it for a moment through the branches. The rim above the ledge looked familiar. He was certain he was right. The scrub oak choked the canyon from side to side at this point, opening out into the alley that had been Spurd's intended shooting gallery. In falling, the rifle should have landed somewhere not far in front of him. But where?

He aligned himself as closely as possible with the ledge

and began to make his way toward the wall. He ran his eyes carefully back and forth as he advanced. He saw no sign of the Sharps. He came up against the canyon wall and pressed his hands to the unyielding stone in defeat.

It had been a tinhorn's desperate gamble to begin with, he told himself, and turned away from the wall. As he turned he saw it.

In falling, the Sharps had lodged in the upper part of a tangle of low evergreen, strangling vine, and spiky bush. Its bulky length seemed to merge naturally with the verdure. Steve uttered a silent prayer of thanks and reached up through the growth to close his hands on the rifle and lift it free.

Its weight felt good in his grip. Hastily he checked its load. He grinned tightly in satisfaction. The load was all right. The rifle had not fired in its fall. It gave him only one shot, but he looked back up the canyon and at the wall above him with a renewed determination. He was armed now, and his enemy did not know it.

He headed back in the direction of the cave, staying just within the brush where it receded from the face of the wall. He slowed his pace near where he had first taken cover. Velador, he guessed, would still be watching and waiting for him to show himself. Steve contemplated his chances. Not even Velador could shoot a bow from a prone position without awkward contortions unnecessary against a weaponless opponent. To launch an arrow he would have to rise partially from concealment. In so doing, he would reveal himself to return fire. But he would not be expecting return fire from Steve, particularly not from a Sharps buffalo gun. Maybe, just maybe, he would be careless.

Steve knelt and studied the canyon. Now, as Velador

had done with him, he needed to outguess his opponent, to anticipate where Velador might be. A long-ago rockfall had transformed the sheer wall here into a steep, jagged pile of stone that offered numerous spots of concealment. An agile climber would be able to ascend it with relative ease. Somewhere in that steep, jagged field of stone, far enough up to give him a vantage point over this section of the canyon, Steve was certain Velador lay in wait.

Steve could not pick a definite spot, but he estimated where he himself might be if their positions were reversed. He settled on a strip of brush-strewn rubble partway up the slope. He eased to his feet, watching that strip of stone for any movement. The Sharps was long and awkward. He held it cocked, barrel down, along his right leg, keeping his left side to the wall. He began to creep forward toward the open ground separating the scrub oak from the wall, as a man who hoped to reach the cover of the wall might do. And surreptitiously he scanned the jagged slope.

He would have to swing the massive rifle up and fire almost instantly. The Sharps was not meant for that kind of quick shooting; Zeke Spurd had proved that in their showdown. And Steve was unfamiliar with the weapon. He had a chance, it was true, but it was not a good one.

He was almost at the edge of the brush now. Surely any watcher on the slope above must have spotted him. He had the sudden, terrifying feeling that he could no longer breathe. Then movement flickered up on the slope. Like a child's toy, almost exactly where he had anticipated, a figure popped into view, arms cocked in the traditional posture of the bowman.

Steve sidestepped, swinging the Sharps up to his shoulder in a single smooth movement. An arrow slashed through the growth beside him. But he had the figure in his sights, at a range that was simplicity itself for the old buffalo gun. Its blast of smoke and flame outdid Alejandro's big-game rifle. Its butt punched into Steve's shoulder like the hoof of a kicking horse. Through the haze of smoke Steve saw Velador go down.

He dropped the Sharps and sprinted out across the open ground to the base of the slope. He went up with thrusting feet and grasping hands, small stones cascading behind him. There was no time for caution, no time to give Velador a chance to recover. In this headlong rush was his only hope of getting within knife range of his foe. As he went up the last section of slope, he yanked the bowie from its sheath.

He burst through a barrier of brush and found himself alone on a flat ledge. At his feet lay a shattered wooden bow with a quiver of arrows. But there was no blood. His snap shot, he realized, must have struck Velador's bow, splintering it. But the slug had been deflected from its target. Steve's head swiveled left and right. Where had Velador gone? Stones rattled to his left. He had a fleeting glimpse of a lithe, near-naked figure seeming to run impossibly along the sheer wall of the canyon where the ledge ended. Velador's fleeing form disappeared behind a jutting rock.

Knife in hand, Steve crossed the ledge. From up close he could detect a faint scar of a trail along the face of the canyon wall. From below it would be invisible. Velador had traveled it with the fleetness of an antelope or mountain goat. Steve cat-footed in his wake, grateful for his hunting moccasins. Without them, following the trail would have been all but impossible.

To his left were only open space and the canyon floor

below. The void seemed to suck at him. The wall, looming above him, appeared to hang over him as if it might at any instant lean farther outward and force him from the trail.

Velador had fled back toward the treasure cave along the precarious path. Ahead Steve saw the path enter into a clump of brush clinging to the cliff face. Velador slipped among a mass of rocks beyond the brush. Steve tried to increase his pace. Then he slowed. Again he had seen Velador. Accident or intention? He thought of that night among the ruins. Velador was only seen when he wanted to be seen. Was the warrior, disarmed now, deliberately leading him on, allowing him to catch those taunting views of his fleeing shape? And if so, why?

Steve recalled the treasure cave, the deadly traps guarding the treasure. He knew his answer. Velador was leading him into a trap, using himself as bait, exactly as Steve had done with Alejandro.

As he pushed through the waist-high vegetation, Steve slashed left and right with the heavy blade of the bowie. Like the short sword Ramon had likened it to, it hewed through stems and branches. And a trip wire. Forewarned, Steve jumped back as the thick supple limb, bent like a bow, lashed around in an arc. The sharpened wooden stake bound to its end drove at his thigh.

It whipped harmlessly past him. Off balance from his backward leap, he teetered toward the brink of the path. The canyon seemed to open dizzyingly below him, waiting to claim his falling body. One wildly flailing hand closed on a heavy vine, and he swung himself back upright.

For a moment he clung there, shaken. But the trap had failed. He could not let Velador elude him. He went forward on the hazardous trail. It took him over the outcropping of boulders where he had last seen his prey. Off to his left on the canyon floor, Steve spotted the horses tethered at the base of the far wall. He realized he must be almost directly above the cave mouth. Silently he stalked forward.

Without warning, the trail emerged onto a wide, flat ledge with a fringe of growth at its edge. Steve recalled seeing the ledge from below, although there, there had been nothing to indicate its surprising size. It was from this site that Velador had undoubtedly fired down on them as they emerged from the cave.

To his right, bulking above him and serving in part to camouflage the ledge, was a crudely made barrier of great logs. They jutted out and up at a steep angle, topped by a great mass of stone fragments and earth and boulders. Steve stared at the barrier. He realized with a sense of shock that he was seeing yet another trap of sorts. And, he realized, Velador had been responsible for that earlier landslide that had come so unexpectedly and almost claimed them as its victims.

This barrier and its mass of debris was the arrangement for a triggered landslide. Now that he looked more closely, he could see the single vertical beam, which, extracted, would let the barrier drop. The dammed-up stone and earth and much of the ledge itself would be sent plunging down the face of the canyon wall, with the cave entrance below in its path. Should that triggering timber be removed, the mouth of the treasure cave would be buried and lost as thoroughly as that of the smelter cave.

Steve looked at the device with awe. Only the rush of displaced air warned him. He sidestepped the fist-sized rock flung with force enough to fracture his skull. He crouched, and Velador, stone ax and gleaming bowie knife bared, pulled up short in his rush. Steve had brought Velador to bay.

Chapter Fifteen

"*H*uuh, Cazador, I knew you would not be easy. I tried to kill you first, but I made a mistake." Velador moved like a stalking puma as they circled. "I knew the other white man would try to kill you. I read it in his eyes that night in your camp. But I believed you would kill him instead, and be the first one out of the cave. But you sent him ahead, and my arrow meant for you slew him. Then the spirits gave you a rifle, and my eyes are old and I did not see it. Now I must kill you with these." He hefted the two weapons clenched in his bony fists.

Steve, his bowie extended, his right side partially toward his opponent, pivoted on his left foot as Velador's relentless stalking drew him nearer. "I did not want this, my friend," he said.

"Huuh. Nor I, Cazador. But you came to the canyon to search for the gold. I tried to warn you. Remember how I told you of the dark spirits guarding the gold? They are with me now, and they will suck your life from you."

"There is only you," Steve said. "You set the fire out on the plains the next night after you came into our camp. You triggered the landslide. You killed Taggar when you had the chance. Not to help me, as I thought, but to warn me, and to rid yourself of one of the intruders. And you set the traps in the cave."

"As I have set them many times," Velador confirmed. "And I have killed many men who came here to the canyon. I have hidden their bodies in these mountains, or sometimes left their bones as a warning to others. My people gave me this duty, and I have honored it. I am sorry now I must kill you, Cazador."

"Your people are gone," Steve said. "It is time for you to relinquish your duty."

"I cannot." There was a sadness in Velador's tones. "I am too old. The years have been too long and too lonely. I cannot betray my people now. I live by the old ways, and they are best. Once, for a time, I used a rifle. But it was a white man's weapon, and at last I threw it away. The old ways, the ways of my people, are all that I have left."

Steve studied the warrior. Velador's movements were lithe and sure. The gnarled muscles rippled smoothly beneath his copper-colored skin. He gripped knife and ax with practiced ease. Velador was no longer the crippled ancient. He was a proud and deadly warrior fighting for his honor and his people.

Perhaps he dropped his guard, or perhaps Velador detected some flicker of regret and uncertainty in his eyes. The old warrior attacked in a swirl of slashing ax and thrusting blade. Steve ducked beneath the arcing ax, parried the lunging knife, blade to blade, with his own bowie. Metal clashed, and Steve felt the strength of the arm behind the blade he parried. He disengaged and thrust in, driving his blade at that lean, fleshless middle. And there was no time for regret or uncertainty. There was only survival against a skilled and dangerous opponent.

Twisting away from the lunge with the agility of a youth, Velador skipped back a single step and drove the blade in his right hand out. Steve parried across his body, his own bowie in his right fist. Again he felt the terrible strength of the old man, even as he realized that the parried thrust had been little more than a feint. Velador swept his right foot around in a low arc. It caught Steve's calf hard, staggering him. Velador let the momentum of the sweep carry him on around in a full spin to his left, hand ax coming around at Steve's chest with all the force of Velador's whirling body behind it.

Off balance, Steve hurled himself desperately backward. The razor edge of the stone ax swept across his chest in a line of icy fire. He sprang back again, aware that Velador had drawn first blood, aware that the Indian brave fought with a style and technique the like of which he had never seen.

Teeth bared in his gaunt face, Velador stalked him, feinting with knife and ax. Steve retreated, knowing his space was limited. The void of the canyon waited at his back. Steve's breath rasped in his lungs. Mere moments of combat such as this could drain a man, sap his strength, leave him weak and helpless.

Almost to the rim, Steve halted. Velador lunged forward almost as if he intended to dive past him. But somehow Velador's legs were entangled in his, scissoring and twisting. Steve fell forward, wrenching his body around so he would land on his side and back. The impact was jarring. Like some great spider, Velador was scrambling atop him, all hard muscles and bony joints. Steve jerked his head aside so the descending ax struck sparks from the stone by his ear. He batted Velador's knife arm away with his forearm, and chopped with his bowie at the brave's spine.

Velador rolled off him to evade the blow. Then they were both scrambling to regain their feet. Coming up first, Steve snapped out a kick that missed Velador's head and caught his shoulder, straightening him with its force. Velador snarled and sprang. Steve's left hand closed on his knife arm, the muscles like hardwood beneath his fingers. The ax hewed around at his skull. Steve's bowie rose to meet it, locking it in stalemate, haft to blade.

They grappled, straining against each other in frenzied effort. Steve felt the pressure of the ax against his blocking knife. For the first time he was aware of the weakness in his wounded arm. Velador's face, savage and implacable, stared into his, the dark eyes seeming to consume him. He realized that the Indian's muscular power matched, if not exceeded, his own weakened strength.

Then the ax slid away from his knife, came chopping down at his leg. Faster, Steve dropped the bowie to meet it. Velador snarled again and brought the ax up and around at his head. Steve's blade met it again, then dropped to slash deeply across Velador's sinewy side.

Velador sprang back, blood already leaking from the wound. Speed, Steve thought with dawning hope. Once again his reflexes had proved faster than those of Velador. Younger than the warrior, Steve realized that he had the crucial edge in speed.

"Give it up, Velador," he urged. "Let us go. If you make me, I'll kill you."

The old Indian's gnarled chest rose and fell as he panted. "If I was not old," he said, "you could not beat me."

Steve did not answer. Perhaps it was true.

Frustration writhed across Velador's face. He lunged with the bowie, slashed with the ax. Steve parried them both, and Velador drew back.

"It is over, Velador," Steve insisted.

For a moment longer Velador faced him in baffled rage. "No!" he cried then with a curious triumph. Both gnarled arms swept up and back, and then lashed forward simultaneously. Knife and ax pinwheeled through the air toward Steve's face. Steve ducked low and saw Velador turn and dart to the vertical timber supporting the log barrier and its burden of stone.

With a wild cry that echoed in victory, Velador grasped the heavy timber and heaved, the muscles beneath his skin writhing and bunching. The timber slewed sideways. Steve saw the great mass of stone and earth poised above him lurch forward as the barrier sagged. Desperately he raced toward Velador.

He saw the old Indian give one last straining heave, saw the timber come loose at last. He felt the great mass begin to descend upon him, even as he flung himself from its path in a diving roll. A great roar assaulted his ears. Above it he heard Velador's startled cry of shocked outrage. The ledge shuddered beneath Steve. Plunging stones pelted him. Dust washed over him in a dry, suffocating fog.

Flat on his stomach, at the very limit of the ledge, he saw the unleashed landslide rush past him, shearing the central section of the ledge from the canyon face as it went. Great slabs and fragments of stone smashed down. Enormous boulders rolled past or bounced far out over the canyon. Steve felt his fingers try to gouge into the trembling stone beneath him.

He turned his head away from the sight and saw another pair of clawed hands gripping the ledge itself, then the dust-smeared visage of Velador peering at him over the rim with wild eyes. In a flashing instant he recalled Velador's outraged cry and realized that the warrior had not made it clear of the landslide he had triggered. Caught by its edge, he had been carried off the ledge and clung now to his precarious grip.

Steve scrambled across the shuddering ground. He was dimly aware that the roar was fading. The worst of the slide had plunged on down the face of the canyon wall.

"Velador, here!" Steve threw himself flat and reached out a grasping hand. "Catch my hand! I can pull you up!"

For an instant those compelling, penetrating eyes held his. Then Velador smiled with what was almost serenity. "Cazador," he gasped, "my friend." Then the clawed hands relaxed their grip, and Velador was gone.

"It has disappeared," Felicia said in wonder. "As if it never even existed."

Steve tightened his arm around her shoulders. They stared at the great pile of stone and earth that had completely obliterated all trace of the treasure cave's hidden mouth.

"Velador or his people must have prepared that landslide as a last resort to protect the cave," he said, "just as they prepared others as traps. When I beat him, Velador realized that it was all over for him. His people were gone. He could no longer perform the duty they had given him. He had gotten too old. So he triggered the slide to bury the cave and us with it. When that failed, and he was caught in the landslide himself, he saw he had no reason left to live."

"He was faithful to his people and his duty to the end,"

Felicia murmured. It might have been the old brave's epitaph, Steve thought.

They had found the old Indian's battered body at the base of the canyon wall. They had buried him there. Steve thought of the treachery and the betrayals that the gold had spawned. In the end, only Velador's motives had been pure. That, too, might be his epitaph.

"Not quite as though it never existed, my sister."

Steve and Felicia turned toward Ramon, who had joined them. With Felicia, he had managed to scramble clear of the slide as it plummeted down to seal the cave's mouth. He grinned now. In each hand he hefted a gold ingot. "Remember? We brought some of these out."

Steve took one of the ingots. He weighed it speculatively in his hand. "A good start for rebuilding the Vendegas family fortune," he said.

Ramon nodded. "Yes," he agreed. "A good beginning. But, of course, half belongs to you, my sister."

"It is better this way, I think." Felicia might not have heard. She had turned her gaze back to the canyon wall. "Captain Vendegas was right when he swore his oath. The gold is better left buried."

"You won't be wealthy," Steve said. "But maybe that's good."

Felicia turned toward him. "What do you mean?"

"When I thought you would be returning to Spain as a wealthy aristocrat, there were things I was afraid to ask you."

"Afraid? What things?" Her brow furrowed in puzzlement.

Steve drew a deep breath. "I thought that a beautiful and wealthy aristocrat would only laugh at a former Texas

Ranger with a fledgling spread who proposed marriage to her."

Felicia gasped slightly. Then happiness danced in her eyes. "No, my love," she murmured softly. "I would never have laughed, not even if I was a rich aristocrat. And I would have gladly given up all of the treasure to say yes. You told me once yourself. Some things are more important than gold."